The Unkindness

OrangeBooks Publication

Smriti Nagar, Bhilai, Chhattisgarh - 490020

Website:**www.orangebooks.in**

First Edition, 2022

THE UNKINDNESS

KESHAV SADASHIV SAPRU

OrangeBooks Publication
www.orangebooks.in

Disclaimer

There are 40 instances of copyright in the book, at 3.26% royalty for The Copyright Holders, the price of the book will be increased by 130.4%, which will then have a 10% increase in price after that, for me. Munshi Premchand's works are now in the public domain according to Indian Law. Outside of these instances of copyright, my work is in the public domain.

AFTER THE CHILDREN

The whole movie is set in black and white. Not necessarily neo-noir, just black and white. Thank you.

The film starts with a police detective sitting in his chair, lost in deep thought. I'll leave it upto the actors or actresses to show how he's being pensive. Thank you.

Deep, deep, deep thought. In fact so deep that all sound slowly vanishes, then all light, and then the sound of the telephone slowly creeps in. Getting louder and louder and louder, until it snaps him out of his thoughts. Since he was protected by his deep thought, the actual sound of the telephone is beyond jarring, it's deeply deafening.

Deeply. Thank you. Now.

He picks up the telephone and speaks.

"Jim, we have an interesting case for you. There's been a victim of a heart attack, but it could be a case of negligence or manslaughter, or even pre-meditated murder, we just don't know. Since she died at sight of the perp. The forensic team found out that she had a healthy body, no history of heart illness, or even the mildest of anxiety attacks. We know this because her medical records show this, psychiatric and physical. She was suffering from depression and neurosis, and there may have been some weakness caused by them, but judging from what we have, it seems unlikely.

The team also knows that she's been dead for 8 hours and that she died before she hit the ground, it seems that the perp put on quite the frightening show"

"Alright Svetlana, thank you. I'll be there in the half hour"

Click

Ring ring

"Yes?"

"Hey, it's me again. I'm sorry, but I forgot to tell you one more detail, in my hurry, and my mechanistic delivery, I forgot to tell you something very important. Jim, it was, huuuuhhh, it was your ex-girlfriend Jim. It was Mary. I'm sorry Jim, again, force of habit"

Jim senses a soft smile at the other end, by the gentle exhale from her nostrils.

"It's okay Svetlana, don't worry, I'll figure this out, it's the least I can do for her" "Okay"

Click

Jim feels really, really grim as he gets up, and gets ready to go out. It's cheesy, but he likes to wear a long coat and a hat, it makes him more comfortable when he's out observing. He smiles.

"*Atleast the perp was physically violent, I mean wasn't physically violent. I won't have to see her mangled or know that she suffered. Thank goodness*"

At the point where he thinks, "was physically violent", he closes his eyes, shakes his head from side to side, and slaps himself on the head. Reset face. Reset Head. Reset Mind.

Jim leaves.

We arrive at the scene of the crime. There's police tape around the body, and white chalk which marks the perimeter of the body.

There's a few forensics who are taking their last photos, and the rest are packing up their gear. Some of them look up and give Jim a nod or smile. Sympathy. He returns their affectionate gaze with a polite look of recognition.

Jim slowly moves into his dream world. The sound drains out, the lights go out. His eyes are shut, his mind blank.

The scene changes. Mary's body is now viewed from the side, as is the floor. Everything around it is still dark. He's picturing the crime scene horizontally, that is on the y axis. She's lying there. She gets up. As she's getting up, the horizontal floor moves from the y to the x axis, and she moves from the x to the y axis. She gently lands at the edge of the floor. Her hair floating gently. Her eyes open slowly. We're back from the dream place. She's there in the real world. We're looking at Jack from the third person close up view. She's blurred in the background, And Jack's still in the dream world. Eyes closed. She walks closer and closer to him, and as she approaches him, still blurred. We close up on Jack's face the world behind him either black or blurred out, her face is close to his, she's gentle, peaceful. She puts her right arm on his left shoulder and kisses him softly on his right cheek. And then whispers into his ear.

"He's after the children"

She looks him intensely in his eyes. He looks at her intently and he has tears in his eyes. He touches her face gently, it's warm to the touch. She closes her eyes, and holds his hand with her hand and rubs her face against the palm of his hand. Just lovingly enjoying his affectionate caress. It's beautiful.

She softly disappears while smiling at him. His hand is in the air, he has tears falling down.

He slowly composes himself. A powerful spiritual experience.

The scene changes. We see him at his home, on his desk sitting pensively. He can't think anymore. He gets up and walks down the stairs to the road. There's a forest on the otherside. He likes the peace and solitude which they provide to him. He lights a cigarette and walks to

the forest. Still pensive. He starts looking around. Then suddenly, the hairs on the back of his neck prick up. He freezes.

He slowly scans the area, walks around slowly. He then, with great trepidation walks up to the boundary of the forest. The camera changes view. It's now looking at Jim. The camera rises from ground level and towers over him, there's terror in his eyes, as he's frozen in place, his eyes wide open, his mouth open, the cigarette falls from his mouth and hits the ground, his face contorts from pain as he goes into cardiac arrest. He falls face first into the soft ground.

The world is dark now, pitch black. We just see his body at ground level. His upper torso. He's in his dream world. Mary walks up to him, bends down and whispers into his right ear.

"Jim, wake up".

He wakes up with a long breath drawn in, his head's pounding and he quickly checks his body for any wounds.

"He almost got you too" she says as he slowly gets up, rubbing his temples. She reaches out for him with a hand.

"Don't worry, we'll get him together"

Jim looks up at her as he's helped up and smiles. The End

Already Human

A bell rings. One of the occupants of the house, a woman walks up to the door and opens it to find another woman standing there.

“Hi!” says the woman at the door.

“Hello, Karya, come in, come in, welcome”. Says the woman of the woman, waving her guest in.

“Meredith, it’s so good of you to have me over, I didn’t know where else to go”.

“Oh, don’t be silly Kari, that’s what friends are for”.

“I haven’t been able to charge either, the way things are going”.

Kari heads inside the house and out to the balcony, as she sits down in a chair to recharge her batteries.

“I’ve been finding it so hard to recharge. People give me these strange looks when I do it, as if I’m not human”.

“Kari, you’re already human”.

Meredith says this as she walks up to the chair near her, and sits in it.

They talk as the time passes, and we leave this world as many others, where being human is just a milestone like any other, and all it takes is for someone to see you like that, inspite of our superficial differences. We leave this story, a tale of longing and belonging, to journey next time, back in the Twilight Zone.

ANA SHEIKH

Song: Salim – Ana Sheikh

Reimagining. More Subversive. More Opulent. More shameless. More Uncut.

1: 0-0:18, 2: 0:18-0:32, 3: 0:33-1:03 4: 1:04-1:15, 5: 1:15-1:26, 6: 1:27-35, 7: 1:37-

1:46, 8: 1:47-1:58, 9: 1:58-2:08, 10: 2:09-2:18, 11: 2:19-2:24, 12: 2:24-2:30, 13: 2:32-

2:42.

1. As he says the first line of the song, "Taal Taal yah habibi, Al khyr maujood, al khyr kiteer", we follow him as he moves to his courtyard of his palatial house. Where he sees 'his' dog and kisses her and cuddles her.

2. The scene then cuts to him in his palatial house, sitting on two people, with one person's back as his support. As he sits on them, he's a hefty person who has three gold bricks on his legs. The people below him are also hefty, and the person who's supporting him as well, as he starts rapping, "Bitch, ANA SHEIKH".

3. "My Money bring me power, ANA SHEIKH, black gold, I send it to the states, young teens, I bring them to my base, bad bitches out looking for my mates; I never say never, ANA SHEIKH, baby if you want bad treasure, call the sheikh, everybody wanna look like the sheikh (true), but they don't have my money, ANA SHEIKH (REPEAT), I can buy anything I want, bitch, ANA SHEIKH, I can buy anyone that I want, ANA SHEIKH".

   It turns black and white and then to colour, as he says, "my money bring me power". He then sprays black gold at the US Flag with a fire truck's pipe from a fire hydrant. He brings all the teens to his base (numbers mind you). Bad bitches (female dogs) are running, out looking for his mates. He then fires a flamethrower at the word NEVER. "Baby, if you want bad treasure". How on the nose should I make this? A male and female sex worker in skimpy clothing surrounded by drugs, alcohol, bacon, etc. give a 'come hither' look to the camera (while lying on their sides with their heads resting on their elbows and giving the come hither sign with their index finger). "Everybody wanna look like the sheikh, but they don't have my money, ANA SHEIKH". Fill up the screen with every baby, man, woman and child dressed up and looking like the sheikh (for reference see the 'Malkovitch Malkovitch' scene from the movie 'Being John Malkovitch'). And then cut back to him on the people he's sitting on, as he fires gold coins at the camera from a coin gun. And as he says that he can buy anyone that he wants, he fires gold coins into the mouths of people (suggestive isn'tit? More like banging people on the head with a sign that reads, "MESSAGE!", but that's rap, everyone, but not a wrap).

4. "You know I can have one wife, two wife, too many, three wife, four wife, too many, five wife, six wife, too many, too many, tooo mannnyyy". At every 'wife' he holds up a flag of (In order): US, NATO, EU, RUSSIA, CHINA, AU (African Union).

5. "OO LA LA! ..." I can't transliterate the rest, but for the 'oo la la' part, it can be similar to the video, as he asks the audience to hold up (na na na na, it's thuh muthafuckin' D-O-DOUBLE G, Snoop Dogg!). And he continues his rap. You got something? I got nothing (although at the namr meh hu sheikh, namr meh hu sheikh, he just continues the hand gesture of 'making it rain', 'cept with monies in his hand, just to make it rain more).

6. Repeat last half of the 3rd sequence in concordance with the lyrics at the point.

7. "I'm a sheikh, sheikh, sheikh, big house in Marrakesh, you know I pay, pay, pay. If you try and fuck with me, you out of game, game, game. Them bottles in the club, they call my name, name, name".

   "Big house in Marrakesh", he's sitting on his slaves again, and gestures with his open palms at the size of his house. "You know I pay, pay, pay". He makes it rain. "If you try and fuck with me, you out of game, game, game". What it says. He fires a gun off in a range, just missing the head of a trussed up human target.

8. He starts going crazy by repeating, ANA SHEIKH over and over again.
9. He's strapped into a chair and jolted with electricity as he stutters Imma sheikh over and over again (in concordance with the song).
10. And he's now out of the chair as he does some rich people antics (see the video where the Russian billionaire shows Colbert how he's one of the 100 people in the world who knows this particular expensive game).
11. "Dollar? Euro? Dirham? Dinar?" As he says this as he points to genuine printing presses of the currency (shipped from abroad of course).
12. Repeat 6.
13. "How much it cost for all your life to make you shut the fuck up? I'd like to pay you to shut the fuck up… thank you! ANA SHEIKH!"
14. He sits on his slave chair as he's speaking to representatives of amnesty international and Greenpeace. Then as the song winds down in staccato beats, the representatives are blown back dubstep style (see the music video of 'Equinox' by Skrillex, when the pedophile/kidnapper is blown back by the bass drop). As he points at them with a lit cigar as he says, "thank you".
15. END.

Inspired from oxventure, outsidextra and outsidexbox.

Sashelas walks into the dark, empty alley between two rows of houses. In his fatigue and in the thick of the night, he feels as if the very darkness of the night is roiling up against the sides of the houses.

He looks around anxiously, walking forward slowly, trepidatiously . As he inches forward, he calls out, “Prudence?”

At this, the dark roiling of the night gets more intense and he hears a whispered, “ehalsweiss” (similar to the whispering heard in the blink ability from Dishonored)

Hearing this, he jumps back startled, his back to one of the walls of the hices (sorry, houses, English is a funny, bunny, punny language).

He then hears the slow rustling above his head and the creepy scraping of nails dislodging grout from bricks.

“Prudence?” he whispers again into the dark abyssal night.

At this roiling gets even more fierce as a wind begins to blow, the trees begin to sway, dark forms appear and disappear in the roiling dark. Fierce but faint reds breaking the roils in their might.

Dark is the night, black is its might.

The man pushes himself further back into the wall, and he starts praying to his God.

Sensing this, the dark grows fiercer and brighter, the scraping gets closer, the red gets redder.

His heart beats faster, the scraping is nearer, the grout rains harsher.

And then he feels it, a sharp nail digging into his left shoulder, then a strange, almost snake-like tongue licks away the blood.

He hears a deep, “mmmmmm” in infernal.

Sharp canines gently grasp at where the nail dug in. Then a slender shape brushes against his body. Soft breasts caress his face, as he feels ridges harden.

A body blocks his view of the night, now only dug in front of him. The ridges rub against his as well.

And then down gently over his manhood. As a figure rises up from the ground in front of him. His vision returns, and a low and husky woman’s voice says, “So, prey, how are you to make up for the lack of my feast?”

As slender fingers slowly close around his throbbing neck. His adam’s apple unable to move properly.

He takes heavy breaths as his eyes water.

“Whew” he breaths out.

“It seems that you will have to satisfy my other hunger in exchange”

“She moves swiftly to grasp his lips within her canines, drawing blood and licking it up”

The roiling brightens to a dull nova, as the two lovers go at it.

BEGONE!

Song: Lochness-Judas Priest

0-1:10:- A man sits at a chair infront of a computer, typing and rubbing his hands (the cold), as slowly out of the darkness, a woman dressed in Black flowing, translucent shawls moves towards him, crouched in a graceful, dance-like manner. She is The Dark Woman.

1:11-1:39:- She grabs a hold of him, his head, to be more precise, and starts to change his actions.

1:40-2:23:- The man starts to play heavy metal very slowly to make her get away. She gets away a but, but not that much.

2:24-6:24:- She starts to sing as she dances, as he continues to play the guitar. They remain within the room. As she lets out a call at 3:30-3:35. the waves travel out.

From 3:39-4:34, a very emotional moment happens. From 4:35-5:27, they get closer and closer, as the World around them slowly begins to shift. 5:28-5:54, the place shifts to a dark land with a lighthouse, as she describes what she sings, as a monster rises from the dark waves of the lake, the clouds are dark with thundering, the monster is the mystery. The people's spirits, retains the empathy, as seen. The woman's hands become a fist, as she talks about them being resilient to discovery, more force, more fierceness, more action. And on and on. 5:56-6:24, The monster rises, when she sings about the Lochness. The music from the man makes her return to a different reality.

6:24-8:37:- 6:24-7:37, as the music builds and grows with intensity and fervour (ferocity), she gets blown further back into different realities. From 7:38-8:07, she cries and implores the guitarist and beckons him. From 8:08-8:37, she becomes aggressive, direct, forceful, confrontational and challenges the guitarist to a duel (this challenge can be humourous if the actress wishes).

8:38-10:26:- Silence, they two are lying together, he's looking down at his guitar, and she is softly smiling and singing (on a rugged black rock landscape).

10:28-11:25:- She pushes him off, and back to the island, with the same scene, on and on!!

11:26-13:24:- The man continues playing. The woman keeps dancing. However she wishes. Some subtle seductiveness, some gracefulness. Fades to black as the camera pulls out.

CLIMATE HUSTLE

A man sits near a woman sleeping on a bed. He's sitting on a chair, facing her. He has a sign sticking out from his head. It says, "Climate Denier". He's holding a book in his hands, which he's pointing at her. The woman's face is painted green.

He says, "Begone, green demon!"

Her eyes open quickly, she glares at him, gets up and slaps a tree into his face with her right hand.

This happens 10 ten times in rapid succession, the same action being repeated as it hits his right-cheek finally.

He flies out of his chair a few feet and does dozens of flips in the air, and crashes dramatically into the floor. His head has trees growing out of it, and the letters in the sign change quickly (like a slot machine) to environmentalist. He has birds and planets revolving above his head.

The woman gets up, looks at the camera and maniacally laughs like the Mask, with a high-pitched, "Ha-Ha!"

The women's legs move very quickly, in one place, as she rockets down the stairs and out the house.

The camera moves to the man's face as he points his right finger up and says weakly, "That worked", and his head flops down again.

As the woman slams through the door, the sight that she's greeted by makes her eyes pop out and her tongue falls to the floor, as her legs lift a few feet off the ground as she screams, "Ahhhhhhhhhh!"

What she sees are as follows:

A looney toon smashing chimneys into the road, which blacken the sky.

An animal torturer, brutalizing all animals in a vicious manner (it's suggested by the horrific noises in his barn, :D)

Government officials handing out certificates which have approved "Destroy The Environment", shaking hands with oily bastards.

Scientists on the ground, having their faces stomped by a boot, which says, "Fuck Science", everytime it stomps a face.

Religious Leaders preaching, "Money, Power, Genocide, Destroy, Obey, Consume".

Judges taking money to condemn the environment and environmentalists to death.

A man sitting on a table which says MEAT, with a fork and a knife, and a maniacal grin.

A man in a chariot, whipping men and women who are pulling it.

Men at the river who are laughing as one burns the birds with a flame thrower, one poisons the fishes, one is spraying brown stuff (shit) from a machine into the river, one is pouring oil from a barrel, and one is using a garbage truck to dispose plastic into it.

Near a bunch of trees, a man is cutting the trees with a chainsaw, and another one is pushing a tree into a grinding, out of whose other end money is flying out.

And a soldier at guard in the centre. Shooting at anyone who gets out of line. People are wheezing and coughing everywhere.

Everytime a bad thing happens, there's an inception BWAAS (air horn) noise. The woman turns the chimneys into windmills, and makes them float in the sky, she zaps the looney toon back to her world, the sky clears and brightens, Government certificates change to "Protect The Environment", Scientists and their torturers are now working together to make the world a better place as friends, The religious leaders now preach, Humane, Kind, Love, Togetherness, Life, Learn, Preserve", The judges and their bribers stop indulging in illegal activities and instead together start to hand out real justice, she turns the MEAT eater into a VEGGIE eater, she turns the charioteer and his slaves into friends in a park, she turns the men in the river to as follows, the flamethrower becomes a lover of birds, the poisoner becomes a bread thrower to the fish, the one dumping brown stuff, into a firemen who douses out the flames, the plastic man, into a flower shooter, with fragrance everywhere, the chainsawer becomes a tree hugger, the money grinder into a gardener and makes the soldier into a happy flowery man, who's holding a big flower instead of a gun, and everyone's smiling and having fun. Whenever something good happens, a twinkling sound plays. Like faeries you know?

As soon as she thinks that she's done, A GIANT drop of oil in a suit, top hat and monocle, with a moustache and towering over everything else, looms over the happy scene, and he starts monologueing. It's oil man!

"I'm the one who's made everyone evil and destructive, Muah ha ha ha!"

Oil-man continues laughing and blabbing, as the green woman starts to rotate her right arm very very fast, blindingly fast. She draws in the powers of Earth, Fire, Water, Air and Heart, she starts to sing the Captain Planet theme song and suddenly, as if her arm is Mjölnir, she flies into the air and destroys oil-man in an instant, and instead of oil, water rains down on everyone and cleans everything, as oil man is destroyed and everyone and everything is saved. Everyone is happy and joyful, as green woman (she isn't actually green) lands and everyone cheers her, and some hug her. Even former denier is seen happy and clapping, as he rubs his cheek and the woman sticks her tongue out at him, as he laughs.

THE END.

Why yes, this is a feel good propaganda film about environmentalism, sharing its name with the drab and witless anti-environment film of the same name, as a tool for awareness and counter-propaganda, love.

Clothes Off

A very seriously dressed man, and a very seriously dressed woman walk up to each other to do some busy work. They look at each other and then they smile, which become really big smiles. Then they take off their loose items of clothing, and then they run towards each other to embrace.

CLUBBED TO DEATH

Song: Clubbed To Death –CTD/Matrix Soundtrack

0-0:25s: The music starts. We see a person in front of a CRT monitor. The camera comes from the rear. Nothing but the computer, and the back of this person's head and the chair that's being sat upon, are visible.

0:26s-2:55m: Our FOV fills up with the following typical montage, Nuclear blast, pollution of the oceans, oil, plastic, coral bleaching, squalor, poverty, suffering, misery, death, destruction, pests (red barnacles) destroying coral, industrial effluence, nukes, acidification, overfishing, bomb-fishing, rivers polluted, death, disease, starvation, famine, drought, evil of capitalism, evil things done to kids, racism, time-lapse footage of Fungi growing over dead corpses, vultures, war, genocide, cannibalism, rioting, civil war, violence, racism, hatred, terrorism, jails, execution, state-terrorism, terrorism on a human level, oppression, etc.

2:56-4:00m: Here. Our Protagonist, a male, any species, preferably human, is fatigued and lays his head down on the table and falls asleep. His face grows old, as he develops a long white beard, mush and hair. Like Jim Carrey imitating Albert Einstein in Bruce Almighty.

As the camera zooms into his face, a tear slowly flows down his eye.

The screen then cuts to blue, as a message pops. "Wake up "three-letter-word", the McGuffin has you". Our protagonist wakes up and looks at the screen. As the horizontal cursor blinks. He blinks back.

The screen sucks him in as he's now in an acid trip. As he heads deep into the computer. Refer to WIWDD by Dan Deacon.

He appears at the other end.

He walks through a dark corridor, with a door at the end. He opens the door and walks out.

Verdant fields and rolling hills fill the horizon. Like an oil painting.

As he's overlooking this beautiful vista of grassy knolls from his vantage point, his father approaches him from the left and joins him. A hand comes up to his back.

It's his dad. He then looks over to his dad, and embraces him in a passionate kiss. This is reminiscent of Winston's dream in the 1984 film "1984".

4:01-5:53: Our FOV now fills up with the exact opposite of the scene of devastation. It is one of regeneration, renewal.

The sixth mass extinction is halted in its tracks, as life makes a striking an uproarious comeback.

All the World's government's fire off their nukes to the moon, and put aside their differences to come under one World Earth Federation (WAIF).

Tribes come under the benevolent state oversight. And all the violent ones put down their arms, to flourish and usher in a new era of peace.

All weapons are beaten into ploughshares. Fulfilling the mandate of the UN.

Famine, death and destruction are thing of past. The Earth, machines and humans co-exist in harmony. Pollution is stopped. The biosphere is cleaned up (Earth, Air, Water, Fire, Heart).

The World Rejoices!! ALL Violence Ends!!

5:54-6:54m: Our protagonist is pulled back out of this World and into the one where he was earlier. Again reminiscent of the acid trip. DDWIWDD.

He takes the VCD out of the FD and places it into its case and snaps it close. On the cover it says, "Reality" (for inspiration, see the album cover of ' Welcome Reality' by Nero).

6:55-7:35m: The protagonist after Welcoming Reality, picks up his jacket and puts it around himself and walks out of the room. As the camera zooms to screen.

It says, "We Are One, We Are Free".

FADE TO BLACK

CRY EVIL

Song: Crysis 2 Theme Song, Hans Zimmer 0-39, 40-1:26, 1:27-2:02, 2:03-2:52

0-0:39: The scene opens with a sort of blurry visual effect, similar to when flashbacks take place in Crysis 2.

In the flashback, a group of men are in Nanosuits, (with their helmets off), having a mission briefing. The camera then changes to the screen on which the data is being projected.
It's displaying some data about the T-Virus.

0:40-1:26: The scene then changes to VTOL craft flying to the Kinshian islands. Here the Ceph are landing with their massive ships. A large number of VTOL craft can be seen, in fact. The Ceph justify the invasion of Earth to protect cephalopods from dying out on Earth, due to the Fallout from human consumption.

1:27-2:02: Lawrence Barnes is morphed into Prophet by the fusion of Ceph physiology with his Nanosuit matrix. Fighting the Ceph in New York and the jungles of Kinshian. But the Ceph keep winning.

2:03-2:52: As governments fall, the C.E.L.L take over the World, and increasingly cease control of resources, with many hostile takeovers. Prophet seizes an opportunity to fuse with the Ceph hivemind. In an attempt to make peace and heal Earth.

As the music comes to an end, and before the screen cuts to black, we centre on Prophet's face (Helmet on).

At the last note, the screen cuts to black, as the film ends.

DEAD ALREADY

Soundtrack: Dead Already (Borjuto), American Beauty OST

The scene opens with a thin man in a kurta, buried in a pile of bodies. He struggles to get free and as he's shuffling through, he finds his mother's body.

The scene then cuts to him being in an open field, with a lake in the middle, trees all around, mountains surrounding the scenery, like a cradle. The sky is full of stars. Even though apparently, it's daytime?

He moves to the lake, and starts eating fruits from some orchards he finds there. He then walks to the edge of the lake and starts to throw rocks into the river. Out of scientific curiosity and ennui. The waves then lap to the shore, leaving big ripples from where the rock splashed into the lake. After sometime as he looks down, he sees a group of tadpoles at the shore. He sees that some of them have died. There broken bodies floating to the bottom (or from the internal trauma caused by the shockwaves, or by their little bodies hitting the sharp, hard rocks at the bottom). He tries to see if some of them are alive, and hopes and prays that they may live. But they don't move anymore, and its body floats slowly a few cms down and comes to a rest. He can't take it anymore and he starts wailing.

The camera cuts back, as a jump fills the frame. Doorless, WW2 era. It comes into view at the entrance of the cradle.

The man sees this and starts to run, but he's too weak, and he stumble, falls and vomits blood.

The soldiers come up to him. They are "Indian" soldiers. Wordlessly, they take out their guns, dismantle them, and throw them into the water (or slide them in, taking inspiration from the scene from Stalker). They show the man that they are unhostile. They offer him a hand and they go back to the orchards, start a fire, give the man some medical care (one of them is a medic).

They eat some food and go to sleep as night falls. We move away slowly from the fire and silhouettes, as we pull away completely to the entrance of the cradle, we see embers in the horizon, red, orange, yellow, all these hues. As we slowly and softly cut to black.

This hints at a global thermonuclear war.

DRAMA

Palying to the song Drama party favor remix with Bro Safari & UFO

0:19 Black man in hoodie gets up from sleep in a start, his head was resting on his hands on a table.

0:36-37 Getup, pushes chair back, and starts walking.

0:54-55 Gunshots fly past him. Everybody around him is panicking, but he's walking calmly. 1:06 Gun Cock. Close up.

1:16 Switch. Gunman(/woman/person/people?) switches weapons (indeterminate race?).

1:25 Gunshot. Kills black man. Black man falls down, headphones fly off, and the music softens in the background.

2:03 Another black man gets up from sleep. Repeat.

2:03 Black man gets up with a start, starts walking. Repeat.

2:23 Switch. Black man picks up headphones and the music starts playing at its familiar volume.

Black man continues walking. Calmly, as everybody around him loses their minds.

3:02-3:03 Getup. Another black man gets up with a start. Another gunshot, close up of the gun. Cut to black. Credits? *Prolonged Shrug*

The black men/man? Are in hoodies loosely covering their heads when they wake up. Properly covering when they/he getup and are/is walking.

DUST TO DUST

1-1:13:- The Earth comes into focus as Mother Earth says, "I am many things, I have been many things".

0:13-0:17:- Warmth and Green is shown as she says, "Warm and Green". 0:17-0:22:- Cold and Grey things are shown as she says, "Cold and Gray".

0:22-0:28:- Devastated and dying things are shown as she says, "devastated and dying".

0:29-0:32:- Growth and Light are shown as she says, "Now I am alive again".

0:33-0:38:- The modern world is shown as she says, "But I fear that my new children imitate the old ones". The post-renaissance, pre-enlightenment era is shown as she says, "the old ones".

0:39-0:42:- Mountains and forests are shown as she says, "some claim the mountains or the forests".

0:43-0:45:- Show massive cities as she says, "Or build fortresses on the plains".

0:46-0:59:- Show authoritarian leaders giving authoritarian speeches and then images of modern total war as she says, "They begin to mistrust, and prepare for war".

1:00-1:04:- Show a mother cradling a baby, as she says, "Still, I love them as only a mother can".

1:05-1:08:- Show a fey creature with small antelope horns dressed in Nature look at the camera, as she says, "And now I fear for them".

1:09-1:17:- Show a gust of wind and then a hurricane, as she says, "I feel the winds of change blow, and this time, it maybe an all-out storm".

1:18-1:23:- Show an aura around the fey creature, as she says, "I pray that my children may weather this tempest".

1:18-1:49:- Show the Earth in profile, as she says, " For nothing is immortal, and one day, they may have to survive without me". After sometime, the Sun begins to enlarge, and the Sun creeps ever closer to devour the Earth, as the music dies down and the video cuts to black before he Earth is devoured.

DUTY CALLED OPT FOR BLACK

Song: Black Ops Theme-COD Black Ops

1-2:05: US soldiers come in on helicopters and take up position behind the charred remains of vehicles. It's New York City, it's WW3, US and Russian forces are fighting each other (you can guess this can't you?). It's very Bayesian (Michael Bay, not the scientist/mathematician, or as it's known more widely, BAYHEM). A US soldier in front of us gets shot in the face as he respawns.

1:06-2:50: We zero in on the soldier who's looking at his hands, as if he's going through depersonalization. "What just happened?" He thinks.

Everywhere around him, bullets are whizzing past, cars are exploding, grenades are flying (XM-25 is that you?), airstrikes, helicopter gunships.

He thinks to himself, "Am I in purgatory? Why am I dying and respawning again and again?"

Thinking this, the screen goes black (blank?), and a pithy comment from some general about some war comes up on the screen. Some red blood twinge on the sides. Oh I know!

"War, War Never Changes" – Fallout 4.

The camera then zooms out faraway, like a killcam from sniper elite (The camera follows the bullet back to the sniper), to a sniper 2 kms away (2km headshot, 4,000 points! Press F to cry). The sniper has a Dragunov.

He gets up and makes fist with his right hand and pulls it down, And says, "Yaas! I'm invincible!" As a helicopter gunship (AH-64 Apache) comes into view and looms in on him. "Oh, Fuck". He says, as his face drops immediately.

Our American Man, respawns again, and angrily shouts across, "Dmitri, you bastard!" "I don't want to shoot anybody!" He thinks to himself (speaks to himself).

"Lots of Russian friends of mine are out there". Then he hears a call in on his radio. "It's Over!"

And then a warning sound (MW2 tac nuke sound) starts playing, "tun-ra, tun-ra".

And then he hears the sound from the Battlefield 2 map, "Strike at Karkand", And then the sound effect from the spawn page of the map plays (also the nuke scene from MW1), "Khwaja Re Re, Khwaja Re Re Kwhaja".

He looks at himself as he starts shaking, crouched behind a burned out car. Palpitations rock his body.

2:50-3:01: And then we cut to the sight of the nuke coming in (for the kill). And then as the woman's voice sings at 3:03-3:10:

BOOM!

A roaring sound and a bright flash as the world around him goes deaf, dumb and dark.

In his thoughts (the screen is black), we hear, "Am I dead?" "No, I'm still trying to move". "Why can't I feel anything?" "Am I in a womb?" He tries to speak but can't. "I have no mouth and I must scream!"

And then as his last breadth leaves his body, the camera pulls out and we see his charred remains, barely any flesh on him, like the dead from Hiroshima, like Barefoot Gen.

As the camera pulls out, the devastation is evident, and then the camera stops, the screen distorts, as the film stops dead due to (data) corruption and it stays like that [the video ends there after staying like that for a few minutes. During this, the tone from the '50s "Standby" sign (which stands for standing by for a signal) plays in the background, or Fallout, whatever is more recognizable to you. This effect registers as the corruption being not only visual, but also audio, and it's also a fun nod to the audience, *wink* *wink*).

(Inspired by the story, Life In The Game, Michael Malkin, 'IF' Anthology, Alterna Comics)

(And of course, Kaal Auf Dooty, has your dooty been called yet? Heh heh)

DYING LIGHT

Based off of the Dying Light trailer (2013) and the gameplay trailer. Song: Run Boy Run by Woodkid

As the music starts (the gong beats), the man looks out over the city form a rooftop, as the sun sets. A flare launches into the sky, marking the safehouse/outpost for couriers. Seeing this, he starts to run. He runs off of the building, into some boards erected for construction, as it cuts to him holding off zombies at a door. He lets go and runs off to the side, into the sewer, as they stumble through onto the floor.

In the sewer (reminiscent of the scene in STALKER where they are in the pipe), the protagonist is running from zombies (running on water which splashes). He reaches a ladder which leads up to the surface. It's already night now. As he runs faster and harder now, his breathing increases, the exertion evident in his face, and in his breathing, a little bit of slow-motion to emphasize this, and now back to normal.

He throws a trap in front of him and jumps over it, as the now ferocious zombies, run, jump, slide, shriek and shake after him. Garrgh!

Some of the zombies step into the trap and get fried. The smarter zombies avoid the trap and continue to run after him. A little later, the outpost comes into sight, as our runs even harder and faster now. His spirit renewed at the sight of salvation and safety. The horde is now even larger and louder, growing with every minute. The lights of the outpost are now blinding, they shine at our hero and the horde. His determination now even more evident. The guards start shooting at the herd to thin it (from their vantage point). As he nears the entrance, the doors open, as the other guards wave him in while covering him.

He dives in as the doors close.

Just before the doors close, he catches a glimpse of the zombie horde. They rasp "Good Night!"

The camera zooms in to the mouth of a zombie with a rotted, toothed smirk, who whispers,

"Good Luck"

EAT COLD CRISPS DOOM MOVIE (20XX)

THEME SONG: DOOM 3 THEME BY TWEAKER

0-44s: The music starts. The scene starts in a Mars facility. We see Doomguy loading up his weapons, especially his iconic super shotgun, Just as we build up to the climactic music, the door opens, and all the demons are before him. Standing in the open Martian landscape.

45s-1m5s: Doomguy fires at the ghouls with his rifle. Shooting bullets and missiles endlessly onto their grisly bodies, as Imps, Revenants and Mancubi all get gibbed to shit and fall before him.

1m5s-1m22s: Doomguy throws away his rifle, and enters Berserker mode. As he moves to eviscerate every ghoul within and without his reach.

(As the singer in the song punctuates his muttering, with oodles of deep bass riffs)

Doomguy rips and tears motherfucker!

1m22s-1m40s: Doomguy runs across the Martian landscape towards Olympus Mons at max speed. The FPV continues, then we cut to a pulled out shot which shows him zipping across the Martian surface at impossible speeds. Then we zoom back to his face; his face is obscured by the helmet visor. But we catch a glimpse of his mouth and face twisted into a demonic grin, ear to ear.

1m43s-1m59s: Doomguy blasts through more ghouls, with his handy super shotgun. Shooting twice with the same rounds, before reloading. Punches out the cartridges, shoves them back in with his right hand, cranks it back in place, shoots, rinse, repeat. BOOM! BOOM! BOOM! BOOM! BOOM!

An endless, merciless assault!

Climbs up to the summit of Olympus Mons, looks down and sees the cyberdemon. Perspective is now lost. Even though the CD is 25kms down, it seems close, real close, especially as the camera zooms into his ugly mug (differing magnification). Doomguy jumps.

2m-2m33s: Doomguy falls down, racing towards the CD. As the shot cuts to the CD's feet, as his boot thrusters fire and he lifts off of the ground and rockets towards Doomguy. Doomguy's boosters also fire.

2m26s-2m33s: They reach each other's fist. Doomguy's left to the CD's right. He's dwarved by the sheer size of the CD. Both are gritting their teeth. The camera matches the staccato bursts of the bass riffs to their fists hitting each other in slow motion.

The title screen pops up as the music dies down. EAT COLD CRISPS

DOOOM IS STYLIZED, OF COURSE.

Same film remade, but this time, with Doom 3 (Simpsonill Remix). And all the entities and surroundings are one mass of flowing, connected liquid metal flavour.

ESCALATION

A man tries to get the attention of his mother, so he takes a particle of dust and throws it at her. He takes his hand and smacks her on the back. He takes a book and hits her. Still nothing. He takes a piece of paper with "Car" written on it and strikes her with it. A truck, A plane, A skyscraper, A supertanker, A Moon, A planet, A Star, A Solar System, A Galaxy, A Supernova, A hypernova, A Quasar, The Universe, BOOM, BIGGER BOOM, BIGGEST BOOM, EVEN BIGGEST BOOM, TOTALLY BIGGEST BOOM,

"MOOOOMM! WHY AREN'T YOU LISTENING TO ME?!"

"Sweetie, all you had to do was ask"

Facepalm

FACE SITTER

Vim playfully trips her boyfriend over onto a pile of cushions, and gently sits down on his chest. With his head between her dress (☺). She rakes her fingers through his beautiful hair, and tells him smiling, “eat”.

FROSTED FLAKES

Song: Frostpunk Sountdtrack, The City Must Survive, 4:07.

0-0:20:- The scene opens on a frozen Victorian City, as dozens of people scurry about frantically collecting supplies in anticipation of something.

0:21-0:30:- People assemble near the generator, now humming with ominous fervor. As they await dire news from their leader.

0:30-0:40:- The worst is to come, the storm is heading directly towards the city, it will be bearing down on us with the utmost of ferocity in 2 weeks. The temperatures are unbelievable even for the scientists, how can something so wild exist on Terra?

0:40-0:51:- People panic.

0:51-1:00:- Calm is restored through order.

1:00-1:40:- But it doesn't last very long, as the leader has to procure vast amounts of coal, food, wood, automatons and clothes. The injured need prosthetics, and so on.

Retreating scouts, outpost groups and refugees report that they see the edges of the storm on their horizons and it is nothing like anything they've ever seen before.

From the distance with their spyglasses, they can see the areas that they just visited, freeze in front of their very eyes, as the moisture in the air flash freezes into ice and frost and encases anything and everything in place.

1:40-2:00:- The resource needs are met and distributed amongst the populace, the coal powered heat generator is powered up to maximum, as all non-essential personnel hunker down in their homes. The Hunter's Hangers are shuttered, pleasure houses, food stalls, places of worship, taverns and almost all workplaces are closed. The doctors and engineers huddle closer to their patients, instruments and heaters. Children are tucked tighter in their in one giant carehouse, with a massive heater to warm them and their parents. All the heaters in all the homes are turned on, flames to last for days in every fireplace are burning, as every soul is waiting.

The only things on the street are automatons. The miners dig harder and deeper, in anticipation of the soul-shattering cold of the storm.

2:01-2:10:- Anticipation builds. The wait, unbearable.

2:12 (pause):- The inevitable arrives, the scientists declare, “The storm has come”. 2:12-2:16: There’s a pause.

2:17:- “Sir, let’s hope that the City survives”. 2:18-2:21:- Pause.

2:22-2:42:- The storm comes and bears down with all its might.

The scientists trapped in their beacon, express shock and surprise as the winds buffet them, they declare through the lantern to the leader.

“-90”

2:43-3:22:- As the temperature keeps dropping with no signs of abating, everything struggles. The people burn wood faster, but nothing seems to push the seeping cold away from them. Heated food freezes, the automatons struggle to move, as the cold makes them brittle, and many brave engineers clad like walruses straddle these metal beasts to fix them. Others still, volunteer to head out in these walrus suits to rescue any of those who may have been caught out in the storm. The leader and his aides brave the storm to steer the heat generator. A dangerous balancing act between explosion and salvation.

3:22-3:50:- As the mines start collapsing under the freeze, the miners abandon their tools, as help comes to rescue them. The temperature drops so low, that nothing, not even those standing just a few feet away from the generator, and say that they feel any heat, as the coldest day of the storm dawns.

3:50-4:07:- And as swiftly as it had begun, so it ends, with a cold whisper, and the entire town breathes a sigh of relief.

GAIA

SEWS outpost 36, Confederation space, Fen Habbanis system, 2396

There are two guardsmen sitting at their posts watching their monitors intently for any signs of incursion. Currently, the heightened tensions between the confederation, the Bright Compact and the Ty'Lneesi Empire are at their highest since the last war in 2178.

Suddenly their monitors light up, and an emergency message is immediately sent towards Gaia, the Confederation home world. And at that very moment, a massive space fleet comes into view. 6 Colossi, 12 Titans, 24 Dreadnoughts, 36 Battleships, 48 Cruisers, 60 Destroyers, 72 Corvettes and a 100 army transport ships.

Within seconds, SEWS 36 is nothing but vapour and dust.

Gaia, Outpost 1,

Heart of Confederation Space, 10 minutes later

"Chancellor Friedrich, our nations have not been at the best of terms since our split 250 years ago. But, I think that now is the time to set aside those differences. The Bright Compact and the Ty'Lneesi Empire represent a threat to the entire quadrant. The Tchaaskerans, the Goxians and the Confederation of Planets all stand united against them. We need your help and the UNE's to protect this part of the galaxy, otherwise both of our democratic experiments will fail, miserably, and we will all become slaves to the Bright Compact and the Ty'Lneesi Empire or be eradicated by the Skanuri Star Destroyers".

"Confederator Ioanna. Very well spoken. But we had warned you, that if the COP broke from the UNE, you would be destroyed. And we have nothing more to say".

"What a pity Friedrich, even after all these years you can't let go of your hatred. How tragic. Nevertheless, whether you participate or not, we will ensure the protection of the entire quadrant. Ioanna out".

Riskamore, Riskamore System, Confederation Space, Same time.

"Admiral Vanthor, hypercomm request from Gaia" "Patch it through"

"Starfleet, this is Ioanna"

Everyone in the entire fleet is at rapt attention.

"I wish to apologize to you. Currently, a massive fleet has amassed in Fen Habbanis. The BC and TE wish to destroy us and our allies and for that I need to ask of you two things. The Tchaaskerans are bravely holding off the combined fleets of the BC in their space. While we and the Goxians will have to hold them off here at Riskamore. I know what you're thinking. Fen Habbanis is our industrial juggernaut, its loss will half our nation's industrial capacity. And yes, we will have to sacrifice the Geqietem system and its 70 billion people. This is the hardest decision I've had to make as my role as Confederator in the last 150 years. Having you attack now to save Geqietem, while vastly outnumbered will leave the entire Confederation open to destruction. We have to wait, the longest wait in my life, while I and everyone in the Confederation will have to hear the screams and witness the horror of this omnicide. The Goxians will take a month to reach Riskamore at Max Warp. In that time Geqietem will be defenceless and it's probable that we will lose all four planets. I have ordered a mass evacuation of the system, but I don't know how many lives will be saved. So, there's a choice which Admiral Vanthor will have to make, both of which will require the sacrifice of Geqietem and your lives.

One, you will enter the Geqietem system and assist with evacuation, but which will lead to your certain death, or two, sacrificing Geqietem, but living to fight another day. I wish I was there with you, I'm here doing nothing, while you'll be there dying. I apologize for having failed you all, all my people. I promised so much and yet delivered so little…

Admiral Vanthor cuts the Confederator short.

"Confederator, if I may. All of us here swore an oath to defend the confederation from the depths of the Panthalassic to the edge of the galaxy for as long as we live. We have no qualms in dying for the Confederation, or for its people. We will cover the evacuation of the Geqietus people, we will hold off the aggressors for as long as we can, or till the Goxian fleet reinforces us"

"Thank you Admiral. Thank you, my brave fleet, the Confederation people will never forget this act, nor this day, nor you. Godspeed Admiral, Ioanna out"

"Attention Starfleet. We will be emergency warping to the Geqietem system. Go to red alert, man all battle stations, divert 90% power to weapons, the remaining 10% and aux power to sensors along with life support. Wear your spacesuits, everyone. Make your engineers Hypercharge your zero-point warp reactors. We're going all out on this! Danger Close formation! Not one ship lost till we get kills!"

Geqietem Quartus Geqietem System That very moment

"Captain, we've secured the planet, the planetary shield is at max power and all the citizens are underground in bunkers. We're as ready as we'll be, ma'am"

"Alright everyone, fall back to your fortresses, the moment those ships come through, we start blasting them with everything we've got"

As she said this, she saw a massive fleet warp into the sky. The Colossus was aimed right at her.

Before anyone could look away, the beam of the Colossus lit up the entire sky and blinded everyone who was looking at it.

Then a cataclysmic quake. A 14 on the magnitude scale rocked the entire planet and nearly tore it apart. The place where the planetary shield building was, was a massive crater a 100 km across, the quake made all the volcanoes on Quartus erupt, starting a volcanic winter. The Oceans sloshed, with massive 3 km Tsunamis which went a 1000 km inland. Entire underground bunkers were reduced to rubble. The ground opened up so much and so deep, that some people swore that they could see magma. The planet was nearly torn apart, and in minutes, entire cities were dust and 15 billion people died just like that.

Through the blinding pain of 3rd degree burns, broken bones and singed eyes, Captain Merzma ordered,

"Anyone alive, report. They will be sending down the armies, we have to destroy as many transports as possible!"

"Ma'am! We have only 2 batteries online! This is the South Pole! We're out of range. The North Pole will be within range!"

"Ask them to reroute all power and put it into automatic! Push it to the point of explosion! We'll atleast get a few of their transport ships, before they destroy them"

"2! To be precise, madam"

"How many soldiers are ready to fight?!"

"All armies are down ma'am, but the entire airforce is airborne, ma'am. But the turbulence is making them lose fighters and AWACS quickly!"

"Ask them to fire all they have at the transports once they're within range! Before the corvettes destroy them! And ask the Navy to fire their Missiles!"

"Yes, Ma'am!"

"What about our nukes?"

"They're down. But the Airforce and the Navy are at 50% capacity, ma'am" "Good!"

"They're within range!" "Fire everything!"

In warp between Riskamore and Geqietem.

"Admiral, we will be reaching the Riskamore system within 2 minutes"

"That's too long, push the reactors as close to self-destruct as possible, we'll do everything else under impulse power"

"Engineering, push to near-self-destruct! Shut off engines as soon as we're out of warp and switch to anti-matter and impulse power. We will enter the system within 20 seconds, sir"

"Good"

They warp into Geqietem.

"Sir, extreme range. We're picking up 50 transports destroyed. They've held off the main invading force sir, but, their entire armed forces have been wiped off. They managed to get one barrage off, that's it"

"Target all weapons at the Colossi. If we manage to destroy them, we may buy the people enough time to finish their evacuations. Target them one at a time."

"Yes, sir"

"If I had my way, I would've warped into them, and then we'd have seen how they liked being outmatched"

"Yes, sir"

"One more thing. Have a Destroyer evacuated and transfer all the fleet's warp reactors to the Destroyer. That'll be our last surprise for the bastards"

"Yes, sir"

"Once I say fire, have us move at ramming speed towards them. We're going to kill as many of them as we can. Set the AI to self-destruct once all remaining vessels have been destroyed.

There's no retreat from this" "Yes, sir"

"Destroyer loaded, sir, all weapons at max power, we're within range of firing" "Ramming speed and fire at will!"

Goxxian fleet Geqietem system 7 days later

"Extreme Range, Uthkxss'Vazxull" "Yes"

"Debris shows 5 Colossi destroyed, 11 Titans, 18 Battleships and innumerable other ships"

"They have left Geqietem Quartus a Tomb World. Geqietem Tertius is being bombarded sir. Their ships are making quick work of the Planet"

"That's it, this madness ends here. Quarzhkull! Fire at will!"

Gaia Outpost 1

1 month later

"Beast Chancellor Ioanna. This is High Emperor Nox. We're willing to settle a Status Quo between our two Empires. Be thankful that we did not use our entire fleet. Accept or be destroyed"

"High Emperor Nox, our nation happily accepts the cessation of hostilities. We look forward to a new cooperation between our nations and peoples, built on mutualism…"

"Stop! Beast woman! Don't defile our Great Emperor and his philosophy. His ears will not be defiled by any beast, least of all a beast woman! Your egalitarian bile and Xenophillic whoring will be destroyed by our empire! You will be cast into the dustbins of history with your blasphemous poison! We will murder all your cubs within our sight! We will carry out a cleansing of your 'Nation' and instead replace it with the stamp of order which is our Empire and the benevolent, just and divine rule of our High Emperor!"

Once the avian was done ranting, his head was severed swiftly by the Emperor.

"I don't suffer insolence, even loyal insolence. So he is now begone to the wastes of his ancestors, where he will fly till his wings fall off!"

"Beast Chancellor, we accept your surrender! This 'status quo' is but a step towards your nation's destruction! Begone Queen-Bitch Whore!"

With that the Emperor cut the connection.

"Verbal insults! Oh whatever shall we do Confederator?!" said Ghuum facetiously. And the entire office laughed.

"Indeed Ghuum, we have humiliated them beyond measure. They will think twice about attacking us Now that even the UNE has signed a defence pact with all of us"

"Ghuum, while Geqietem and Fen Habbanis are being rebuilt. I need you and your excellent science vessel. G'thor the Unimpressed to travel to the Geqietem system and bring back research for upgrading our technology and rebuilding our fleet. When you come back, I want to aid with research along with all our other science vessels. The next time they attack, I want our fleet to overwhelm there's!"

"At once Confederator!" Archived at Memory Lambda. 6196

The Galactic Confederacy.

GODZILLA

The Earth. From space. Calm, serene, peaceful.

A massive explosion appears into view from the North-Western United States, as the Yellowstone Caldera erupts.

Slowly, from the monsterous plume, a giant emerges. King Ghidorah. Standing 15 kms tall, with a wingspan of 25 kms.

Far away, at the Japanese side of the Pacific ring of fire. An equally massive volcanic eruption triggers a chain reaction , as all the thousands of volcanoes erupt simultaneously, as does every other remaining volcano and supervolcano on Earth.

From this steaming pit of lava and steam, Godzilla, standing 5 kms tall, emerges and starts moving towards the Californian coast, as they are inexorably attracted to one another.

All of Japan is flattened and flooded by kilometre high waves, which will soon be the case for the hundereds of millions of people who will be sundered into the waves across the coastlines of the World.

Meanwhile in America, the ash cloud covers most of the continental US. As Ghidorah moves towards the Californian coast.

Massive clouds of ash and major forest fires blanket the Earth, as the planet slowly comes under the icy grips of a Global Volcanic Winter.

Even before these behemoths fight, they have doomed civilization.

Every step an Earthquake, every roar a volcanic eruption, every breath a hypercane.

Their slow motion battle rages.

Ghidorah's laser breaths lash Godzilla's ethereal armour.

Godzilla's giant atomic breath, fires with the force of megatons. Every second, the energy of one Tsar Bomba is released.

Ghidorah is surprisingly unfazed by this show of force.

Ghidorah's space armour is impervious to Godzilla's devastating atomic breath. Godzilla's Earth armour is brittle to his Gaser attacks.

Their fight makes the air, hot plasma and the ground beneath them, corium.

Finally, Godzilla faced with defeat, lunges towards and body slams Ghidorah to the ground.

An eldritch Earthquake makes the World shudder. Godzilla Self-Destructs.

Instantaneously, a fireball 50 kms wide and tall incinerates everything. The gargantuan blastwave destroys any nearby mountain range from the bedrock.

The cataclysmic explosion ejects trillions of tons of rock, magma, ash, enormous radiation and various poisons into the atmosphere.

Only to come down and incinerate the atmosphere.

The icy cold volcanic winter gets colder and darker, as the world descends into a icehouse state not seen in more than half-a- billion years.

100 years later…

Despite the apocalyptic events of the fight. Life swiftly makes a comeback . The scars of the battle now covered under thick canopies.

“Great-Grandpappy, where were you during the fight?”

“Well, your great-grandpappy… was shoveling shit in Louisiana”. 66 million years later…

The distant descendants of man and other species rediscover the fossiled Uranium lines marking the fight. Of particular interest is the urban strata of prehistoric man and giant, mountain skeletons.

Despite their vastness and might, time grinds all to dust. And it ensures that the meek shall alwys inherit the Earth.

As this is done, an Alien from the sky sees Godzilla dancing.

“A happy moment”.

☺

HOW TO PREPARE FEET

The scene opens with hot water being poured into a bucket. Then there's a person sitting on a bed, who puts his feet into a tiny water holder (don't know its name). Ahhhhh.

Then it cuts to two people sitting on a table being served feet soup. "Your feet soup sir"

"Thank you"

They each take a sip of the water.

One person exclaims in a terrible British accent. "What a footjob!"

INJUSTICE IS HUMANE

Outside a Jhuggi-Jhopri, Gheesu and Madhav are seen sitting, facing each other. Inside the house, Gheesu's wife is in the process of giving birth to his child.

"What do you think, dad, do you think she will survive?" Gheesu asks his dad. "What're you saying, beta, of course she will come out alive" He replies.

"I don't know dad, I feel that there has been so much injustice and sorrow in our lives, that even thinking about happiness makes feel like as if she will run away".

"Madhu, happiness is a state of mind, it's a thought. Look at Khocher, he's an invalid, and he can't even speak, but even so, he stays happy".

Upon hearing this, Gheesu feels very irritated.

"Don't talk to me about Khocher, papa, he's always high and he always keeps his sorrows locked away in his drugged out mansafe".

"Arre Beta, think from a soft heart, in his life, in our lives, there was nothing, there is nothing, nor will there be anything. At least this way that poor soul can find some happiness, and so can we".

"Papa, in my life, my happiness is lodged inside you, Priya and our child in her womb, without you all, my life would be destroyed, my love would be buried in a cemetary and my humanity would be orphaned".

After saying these words, Gheesu became quiet, and a heavy silence fell on and between them. His words hit Madhav's heart like arrows.

After sometime Madhav speaks and says, "Beta, I just wanted to make you a little happy. You will never be orphaned, I will never leave, God would never let such an inhumanity, such an injustice win over humanity and justice".

"But papa, injustice is humane".

"We don't cry, suffer, impoverish, destroy, kill, beat, etc. things, we only do this to human beings, because their response is similar, is familiar".

Madhav on hearing this, starts punching his head with his hands, and starts keening with grief. Seeing this, Gheesu reaches out to him to stop him, to comfort him, but Madhav slaps him. Gheesu is caught off guard by this, and he just gawks at his father with his mouth open, he had never slapped him ever, never even raised his hand on him, before this.

"This kind of despair will only happen when I die! You stupid cunt!"

Madhav now had tears in his eyes. They were rolling, streaming down his face. Gheesu hugged his father head, as he pressed to his shoulder, and he started to rock back and forth.

"Forgive me, beta, I understand your sadness, even I am wrought by despair". "Papa, forgive me as well, you were just trying to make me happy".

Gheesu looks into his father's eyes as he wipes away the old man's tears from his eyes.

"Priya will give birth without any difficulty whatsoever, we will have not have one but uncountable children, you will make a great dada, and I will never be orphaned".

Hearing this Madhav couldn't help but laugh out loud with great mirth and joy. And they both started to bawl with laughter, as tears roll down.

And just a little later, the door of the house opened and out stepped a woman, well, actually, she was just half out, well, actually she just poked her head out. And a woman's voice called out, "You can come in now".

They both looked at each other, and got up to go in. END

MEGA ENCORE!

Song: Encore by Eminem (2004)

I leave this to the director and the rest of the crew of how to play this out.

Put simply. This is a movie to bring together the seemingly disparate world of the left and the right together again

(Make Earth Great Again. MEGA. Beat that Trump! He's fake! Mine rolls off better! What would you like to say? MAGA or MEGA! Which sounds more epic? I say that MEGA does! Heck we should call this MEGA! I have the best acronyms! The best! We will make Earth Great Again, starting with better coinage! It always sucked to me how we had the worst coins. Stupid! Coins! Now, we will have the best, the best, the best that I like, Gold! Gold coins! Forget golden showers (lies!), it's now Golden coins, fuck yeah! And even better! The OOILL will make it! Then they'll stop being rapists!)

Play the song, listen, figure something out and then when Eminem says, "all my people to the left and the right swing one last time" .

Simple, to solve the Earth's problems everyone must come together, regardless of colour, creed, affiliation, nation, etc. We must put outside our differences and Make Earth Great Again!

EARTH FIRST! EARTH FIRST!

#MEGA!

MIND SCREW

A Draugen game lemon. Autoerotica.

Edward on the left Lissie on the right

“Lissie. You and the Angel said to me that you two will always be there for me” “I did say that old bean. What’re you getting at?”

Edward moves closer to Lissie.

“Do you think that I could, that you could, that we could pleasure each other?”

“I am your ward Edward, even though I’m only a figment of your mind, I am still real”

“Oh”

“Yes Edward. When we said that we would be there for you, I hadn’t counted on this”.

“How come? You are me.”

“I know everything that you know. But I know things more when you admit them to me”

“When you masturbate, do you think of me?” “Yes”

“Oh, Edward” Lissie rubs his face.

“And what about you, Lissie?”

“Edward, I don’t manifest till you wake, and only when you wake”.

“What about in dreams, Lissie?”

“That’s upto you, Edward. Maybe when you’ve passed out from drinking too much noodle soup, perhaps it will be something you dream of. But, in a way, whenever you pleasure yourself. We pleasure ourselves”

“True, that’s true, Lissie”.

Edward then goes back to his work and drinks his noodle soup (tea). And he passes out. And the rest is history.

"I'll always be here Eddie".

MUMMY

To archaeologists walk up to a newly discovered entrance of the pyramids of Giza.

"Huh, well, this is new. The scans revealed this corridor, hidden from sight. We mapped it with Doppler, so we should be fine" said Bob.

"Okay" replied Amy as they both walked into the pyramid.

As they moved into the corridor, the lack of the familiar musty smell, alarmed them for moment. Grave robbers got here before them. But, no, the wind started to move and the familiar smell came back and they started to walk in further.

Being experts on ancient Egyptian, they were always interested in the hieroglyphics that lined the walls, but curiously there weren't any here.

"The poor bastard must've been unimportant as fuck" echoed Amy's voice. "Huh? Yeah" grunted Bob.

They walked what seemed for ages. But they soon came across an entombed mummy. "Akhenaten, the unbidden. What a freaky name for a dead guy"

"Yeah. Dying unadorned, forgotten, not even a motif, oh well" "We'll place a marker here for the team to pick him up" "Yeah"

They kept walking, and walking and walking, for what seemed years, to no avail. There seemed to be no exit. Not even a fart of a wind, pointing towards and exit.

And then, Bob felt a finger tapping on his shoulder. Whisper shouting, "Amy, what is it?"

"Nothing" "Really?"

"Yeah"

"Then stop tapping my shoulder" "I'm not"

And then raggedy words as if from a deflated bag pipe spill out. "There"

And just before Amy and Bob run for their lives, they see it point to the corridor on their left. "Thank you!"

And Bob and Amy run till they see the light, and out they fall 4 feet into the hot sand, bruised but alive.

"I'll ask the air force to blow this pyramid up forever!" "Yath" Amy says, as sand falls out of her mouth.

NOTHING BUT YOUR SOUL

The Soviet Union walks down big steps, as the 'most epic version of the soviet march of all time…ever' (yes, that's its name) plays. A soldier carries the Soviet flag. Stalin looks proud and majestic. Adolf Hitler walks up the big steps, as the song, 'Hearts Of Iron 4-Axis Theme' plays. The soldier behind him has the flag of the Third Reich. Hitler also looks proud and majestic. Hitler points to Stalin (as if giving the 'sieg heil' salute, so Hitler is a bit below Stalin, so that it appears that way), and the soldier from the TR attacks the Soviet soldier (as the song, 'HOI4- Operation Barbarossa' plays). Stalin then points to the German soldier while mouthing the 'Not One Step Back' in Russian (as the song HOI4-The Great Patriotic War plays). On the other side, Churchill is seen walking up to the left of Hitler, and is pointing to him, as a British soldier with the Union Jack is attacking another German Soldier ('HOI4-The Royal Airforce' plays). Mussolini is standing below Hitler and is pointing towards both the Soviet Union and the UK as Italian soldiers attack both.

The camera pulls away to Japan. As Prime Minister Tojo is shown pointing towards The Second United Front (Communist and Republican China and their soldiers with their flags. Mao and Chiang Kai Shek, respectively, as HOI4-Bring Forth The Tanks, along with HOI4- Battle Of Wuhan for the Chinese) and towards America (Eisenhower and an American soldier carrying the Star Spangled Banner, As HOI4-Empire Of The Sun plays for the Japanese side) on the other side.

And America points back (as HOI4-Allies plays, should've called it 'Beacon Of Democracy', just saying).

All the soldiers look proud and majestic as they point towards their enemies.

All around them there are civilians who die. And soldiers who die with fear, determination, resignation or pride.

Everything slows down as the camera slowly pulls away and pans around them (as HOI4- Hearts Of Men plays).

And then the screen slowly fades to black (Then HOI4-The Children of WW2 plays).

This is a way to show the futility of the Second World War. How tragic it was that everyone died. Things that modern retellings oft forget. That this war was as tragic as The Great War (WW1) if not more. People have no compunction to frame that as a tragic mistake. That is the same way that WW2 should be framed as well. Attributing excessive heroism and jingoism towards WW2 risks a repetition of that conflict. It should be reflected as the tragic mess that it was.

Let us not forget so that it is never repeated.

POWERED DOWN

A man walks up to what looks like a government building. And walks in. There's a woman sitting at the front desk.

"Is the Panchayat in?" "Yes"

"May I see them?" "Yes, please follow me"

The man and the woman walk down a corridor and stop at a room at the end of the corridor.

The woman knocks at the door.

"Come in"

"Ah, yes, what is it?"

"Sir, this man has come to see you".

"Oh, it's you. Come in. Thank you"

The woman leaves as the man enters.

"Aftab, it's a real pleasure to see you again. Will you take something?" "No, thank you, I've just come for the factory".

"Ah, always straight to the point, aren't you?"

"Yes, that's how I am"

"Well, tell me what I can do?" "I've got some land in Lar" "Yes, so I've heard"

"Please!" The man speaks agitatedly.

"Let me finish"

"I wish to make it into a chemical factory" "I'm sorry, I can't allow that"

"It would pollute the soil and the water, and make my people very sick. I hope that you can understand"

"Maqbool"

The man leans in.

The Panchayati Raj sits up straighter as Aftab calls him by his real name.

"We've known each other since we were kids. D'you really think that I would endanger this village?"

"These are my people just as much as they are yours"

"I will take all the necessary precautions that are required for a chemical factory. In fact, I will adopt Western standards".

"What American, or European?" "German"

Maqbool gives Aftab a long, hard stare and then says,

"Okay"

"Okay"

"What do I need to do?" "Sign this paper"

"You know that I can't read or write, right?" "I know, I know"

"But, all that this says is this, 'I, Maqbool Khalid, Tehsildar of Lar, hereby allow Aftab Fakhri to build a factory for the manufacturing of detergents on his property. I hold him responsible of any and all his actions, by the power granted to me by the state of Jammu, Kashmir and Ladakh and the government of India. Any violation this agreement, whereby the people of Nadi village or any of its neighbouring villages come under any kind of harm whether direct or indirect through the functioning of this factory, this agreement shall be null and void and his property shall be seized by the state'".

"Okay"

"I trust you, but remember, I'll be watching".

"I wouldn't expect anything less" Aftab smiles softly.

Maqbool signs the agreement and Aftab shakes his hand and walks out of his office. He looks to smile and wave goodbye to the receptionist, but she's not there. He shrugs. We see him walk out of the building.

Sometime later, after Aftab has started his factory , he suffers a heart attack and dies. He is succeeded by his fellow business partner, Altaf.

Altaf, unlike Aftab is unperturbed by the agreement, and wishes to make as much of a profit as possible, he fires the safety staff, removes the electronic monitoring system , orients the wastewater pipes to the river, fires the permanent workers and hires temporary workers from different parts of the state and the country.

Unattached to the village and the land. First. The workers who are closest to the wastewater, start falling ill, then the people in the village.

Maqbool hopes that this problem can be solved by waiting Altaf out and by using diplomacy, instead of just seizing the factory. After all the factory brings jobs and boosts the local economy.

But, one day, he is informed by phone that his pregnant daughter has been hospitalized due to severe heavy metal poisoning. The time to wait has gone.

Sensing the increased urgency of the issue, Maqbool rushes to Altaf to confront him.

He pleads with Altaf to improve his standards, or he will be forced to seize the factory. He even offers to buy the factory from him. But his asking price is far too high, Maqbool heads back empty.

People in the village, sensing no change in the status quo, decide to take matters into their own hands. They begin to protest outside Altaf's factory, but after weeks of protest and media attention, Altaf refuses to step down.

Then one day, in the night, a youngster runs upto a street light and notices the switchbox adjacent to the light. He pulls the lever as shouts are heard from the compound.

"The power's been cut, go check it out!"

The youngster runs towards the rear wall, in the relative dark. He throws the gasoline tank over the wall and then scampers over it.

He falls face first onto the grass and cuts his lip badly.

He cradles his face for a little bit, and then gets up to spit the blood out. He picks up the petrol tank.

Near him is a red sign on a rectangular building. He guesses correctly that this must be where they keep the chemicals.

He quickly unscrews the canister and then proceeds to open the window, pours out some of the canister's contents on the workbench and then just drops the rest of it on the workbench. He then lights a matchstick and chucks it onto the fuel soaked workbench. As he does this, he hurries back to the wall and scampers back up it and makes well sure to not to smash his face into the ground again. He quickly runs away, as small explosions make the flames leap higher.

The firefighters come late to the fire and when they're finally able to douse the flames, nothing was left of the building.

Altaf faced with massive losses, leaves the village on the bicycle that he came to it with.

Maqbool is fired from his job due to his gross incompetence, and goes back to his old farming life.

On his way out of the government compound which has been built adjacent to a temple.

He tries to ring the bell, but it's far too high and it exhausts him

"Who builds temples so high?"

At the compound there's a police officer who sits guard with his head resting on the lathi.

Occasionally a tuk-tuk passes him by, as a chaiwallah walks over to give him tea and biscuits. They have a cordial exchange.

The factory grounds lie empty, as plants begin to reclaim the land.

THE END

PREDATED

DEEPEST DENSEST DARKEST DANKEST

Dutch and his team are clearing out the compound of the guerrilla's in Central America.

They reach a reed door, and instead of knock-knocking, they deliver a grenade right up their alleys.

"Time to change the wallpaper!" shouts Dutch as he thrusts the grenade launcher through the door and the grenade flies out and explodes in mid-air. Everybody in the room dies, horribly eviscerated. There's no need to be graphic, just the lower parts of their fallen bodies are shown and horrible amounts of blood on the walls and ceiling.

Dutch leaves with his team. A little later. The Predator comes across the carnage. He reaches the room where the grenade exploded. He approaches what appears to be what remains of a woman. He scans her with his thermal imaging.

He finds a shrapnel embedded in her stomach which has impaled a nascent foetus. The Predator roars in anger and runs off to find those who did this.

REAR ENDED

A man moves to eat another man's behind. An audible "prrrbbbtt!" is heard. The man turns his face away from the other man's buttcheek, as they both start laughing.

RESIDENT EVIL MEGADEATH

What the name suggests.

(This film assumes an alternate reality where US infrastructure, planning and logistics are at their best)

This script will be a different beast. It will contain scenes from the beginning, middle and the end of the movie. But the director and the rest of the crew will have to fill in the blanks, by using their creativity. As I have no clue as to how I will finish this.

CAST

Chris Redfield | Jonah Scott Annette Birkin

Claire Redfield | Others (additions)*1 William Birkin Jill Valentine | Leon .S. Kennedy

Barry Burton | Lawrence Barnes*2 Private Jonah

Rebecca Chambers | Doctor Mendoza Sherry Birkin | Commander

Flynn | Brad Vickers

Lisa Trevor | Extras (Docs, nurses, etc.)

Depending upon how the gaps in the script are filled in.

Lawrence Barnes is a fun Easter Egg from the Crysis series of games (by CryTek). Are they in the same Universe? After all Prophet's (Lawrence Barnes) first mission does take place in 2020 (Crysis Warhead). Could this be his backstory? Is the T-Virus the precursor to the nanobots seen in Crysis. And could this, his first encounter with it what proved to be his selection into the Nanosuit program? His genetic compatibility with nanobots created by contact and gained immunity to the T-Virus? Who knows? Let the fan wars, flame wars begin! Let fan theories abound! Booyah!

I'm so sorry, but I just can't say the word DOOOOM, without making it sound epic and ominous. Blame DOOOOM and Bethesda. DOOOOOM. *Metal Riff Follows*.

Sabot rounds are Steel Rounds Shaped like a Torus (doughnut) with a sharp cone at the front end, with a magnesium core which burns at 3,300+ degrees Celsius (6,000 degrees

Fahrenheit) during and after the explosion (think of it as high-heat napalm with fragmentation, instead it's designed to punch through MBT armour and not organic matter).

SCRIPT

The title screen drops as how it does in the 2019 remake of Resident Evil 2. Every word with a respective bass beat (I think, see trailer for reference).

The movie opens with the S. .S helicopter flying over the bridge which leads to Raccoon City.

Inside the helicopter.

Crackling radio

"Overwatch! Come in Overwatch! This is Big Bravo Omega Sierra Sierra! Do you read, over?!"

Flynn: "Big Bravo, we read you loud and clear! Over!"

"Oh thank God! We finally got in touch with you. Be advised, zombies are overrunning the city. Stay away from the hospital and other emergency services. If you need security or medical help, reroute to the STARS regional hospital at the outskirts of the City"

Flynn: Roger! Rerouting. Alright folks, looks like the city is unwelcome. Hold on to your butts!

The helicopter banks hard to starboard, to head to the south-eastern part of the city.

The camera cuts to a car on the bridge to Raccoon. Inside are two women. Claire and Ada.

Claire: Hello, Leon? It's Claire, I've got Ada Wong next to me, she was the one that I told you about who wanted to spill the beans about -.

Leon: Claire, I'm going to have to cut you short there, I have an emergency call which I'm responding to.

Leon puts the phone down. Claire hears the disconnect tone. Claire: Okay, looks like your story will have to wait.

Claire looks to her left and comments on the jam.

Claire: Strange, I never expected such a rush to leave the city, it's not even holiday season, or am I missing something?

Ada just stares off into the distance with her forehead pressed against the window, she looks apprehensive.

The scene cuts to the helicopter flying towards the (STARS) hospital. As they fly above the city, Flynn notices the smoke, jams and crowds of people running.

Flynn (sarcasm): What's going on? There's pandemonium on the streets. Did the Mets win, or is there a mass shooter on the prowl (he remarks darkly)?

Brad (looks at Flynn with a thin smile): Funny.

The hospital comes into view at the south-eastern edge of the city. The pilots can see the large number of people milling about, hurrying to do their duty. They also notice the presence of the US National Guard and the US military.

Flynn (looks back at the rest): Something big is going down, boys and girls. They called in the big guns.

Chris and Jill walk to Flynn and peak out of the windshield to look at his view. Aside from the large number of people running about, they notice the presence of APCs, Humvees, Blackhawks, Hueys and other materiel. Reminiscent of the scene from Godzilla (1998).

Jill: Are you all thinking what I'm thinking?

Flynn: Yep. Zombie apocalypse. Get ready to fuck your brains out guys and gals, it's the last chance you'll get. You done? Good.

Is this far too much sarcasm? Or far too much sardonicism? Oh well. The helicopter lands on the makeshift helipad.

Chris, Jill jump out, as Barry and Rebecca gently pull Lisa out on a stretcher and take her.

Flynn (looks in their general direction): Well captain, we'll look after the ship for your return. **(Looks at Brad):** Ship's mate, get your ass out, we got some work to do.

Brad smirks and gets out (his ass, of course, what else? Yes, we're being literal for the sake of humour, but only on this paper, not real real life, of course, right?).

Barry and Rebecca head for the med station in the red-cross tent. Chris and Jill head for the command tent.

In the med tent, as Barry and Rebecca set down Lisa on the floor, as there are no free beds. Many of the patients lying in the beds are in various stages of bandage. Quite a few of them are crying out in pain, as nurses and doctors attend to them. Barry hears a gunshot not faraway and so rushes away to check the source of the sound. Luckily, Lisa doesn't need field surgery, so Rebecca doesn't need Barry around. Nevertheless, she still needs intensive care. She cleaned her up sufficiently in the helicopter, now it is time to care for her better.

As Barry rushes to the sound of the gunshot, he comes across a partition in the tent, marked 'morgue'. He enters, and sees a young doctor holding up a pistol

(M1911) slowly taking aim at the dead bodies and shooting them in the head. Clearly she's a noncombatant in every sense of the word, as she's shaking and her grip on the gun is unsteady.

Barry (comes upto her and gently takes the pistol out of her hand as he comforts her with the other): Let me do it.

Barry takes the gun and asks her to leave the tent. He checks the ammo and places the magazine back with a click. He continues the job of shooting the bodies in the head. The doctor as she's walking towards the patients in the med tent, cringes with every shot she hears.

Chris and Jill have now reached the command tent, and as they enter, the commander (in my imagination a black actor), is barking orders all around. Verbally, through the radio, physical gestures, the whole nine yards.

They come across a soldier running past them, and they stop him. Chris: Hey, **(*checks name*)** Chris, d'you know what's going on here?

Chris (not Redfield): Zombie Apocalypse, Government mismanagement, Umbrella assholes, city evacuation, Army stretched. Busy.

And he walks past them.

Commander: You over there! Yes you! Gormless! Get over here!

Jill: Commander, what's the situation?

Commander: The situation's FUBAR! That's what it is. I have 20,000 men, but it doesn't mean shit when half of a 1,000,000 strong city is ready to rip our fucking faces off, and the media is ready to scope up our asses for every kill. **As he says this he chucks down the file he was holding.** Luckily, the government has a contingency plan for a zombie apocalypse, but it isn't worth spit on a spotted dick. It's basically, contain, evacuate, pull out and hammerdown.

Chris: Tactical nuke?

Commander: If that's what you can call a 1 megaton nuke, son.

Jill And Chris: Fuuucckk.

Commander: That's what I made very clear to the president. I need you here, in this city, help as you can, and then pull the fuck out with the last few evacs. We send the rest to the cold war fallout shelters. Some men inevitably die, that's life in the Army, son. We're expendable, but American citizens are not. Within reason. We evacuate whoever we can.

We only have 24 hours, and by tomorrow this time, Raccoon City and the surrounding 78 square kilometres will be glass. Now get out! Enough chit-chat, we have a city to save!

Chris and Jill get the fuck out, just in case the next file was aimed for their heads.

As they walk out, they notice two cars rolling in. One's a cop car, and the other's civilian. It takes Chris a moment, but he recognizes his sister, and some other random ('Asian', in American parlance) woman sitting next to her.

Chris calls out to his sister, and she notices him and waves towards him. Then she shows him a finger, symbolizing, 'wait'. Then she walks towards the cop car and starts to help what appears to be a badly injured girl bleeding profusely (who's in her parent's arms). The Asian woman in the car steps out and also walks towards the cop car to see if she can help. Two officers step out of the vehicle and gently take the girl from their hands. They carry her over to the tent marked with the red-cross insignia.

Claire comes over to Chris and gives him a tight hug. And without saying a word she runs over to the med tent. Jill just looks at Chris, and Chris just looks back at her, and they give each other a shrug. Ada just looks about at a loss, and finds a chair to sit down in.

Inside the med tent, as Rebecca is done stabilizing Lisa, and Barry is done shooting the dead bodies. As they look up they see the cops walk in, and they see a dead girl in their hands. From faraway, the good doctors can deduce that that girl is dead. But of course, being good doctors, they can't discount on the small chance of saving her.

The cops place her down gently on the bed, as Barry and Rebecca rush to help save her. To save on details, they do their best doctoring, and try to help her as much as they can. But it was too late. Her little body couldn't survive the strain of the massive blood loss she faced.

Barry: We can't just shoot a little girl in the face, when her parents are around.

Rebecca: And what about when she turns?

Barry: We'll cross that bridge when we reach it.

Rebecca: And what of when she becomes a threat to everybody else here?

Barry: Restraints?

Rebecca (turning to the doctor in charge): Doctor?

Doctor: Mendoza.

Rebecca: Mendoza. Are there any restraints in here?

While they are talking, Claire who is already present here. Turns towards the cops and asks.

Claire: You're cops, you must have handcuffs?

Lawrence Barnes (Leon's partner, turns to Claire): Yes. Right here.

He hands his handcuffs to Claire. Claire: Thank you Lawrence.

Lawrence: Doctor, we'll stand outside. Call us if you need us, we don't wish to crowd.

Mendoza: Yes. And that goes for you to **(she looks to Claire, as she takes the handcuffs from her).**

Leon (Steps forward, offering his handcuffs as well): Here, take mine as well.

Mendoza: Thank you.

Mendoza (turns towards Rebecca): Here, now we do have restraints **(smiles). Barry:** You're taking shooting people in the face really well.

Mendoza: Well, as a doctor, I do have to do uncomfortable things. And they weren't people, they were bodies. Makes it easier. Although, I'd have to hate to speak to the families.

Barry: If they're still alive.

Mendoza: If they're still alive.

Mendoza: I'm distancing myself right now. But once this is over, I don't how I'll feel, I'll be a wreck, that's for sure.

Leon and his partner walk out of the tent. Mendoza hands over Leon's handcuffs to Rebecca and Barry. Barry and Rebecca then move to help Doctor Mendoza with whichever patient she needs help with after placing the restraints on Sherry.

Claire walks out towards Chris and Jill, as William Birkin (the girl's father) walks past her hurriedly towards the tent.

Claire goes back to where Chris and Jill are talking and finally talks to them.

Claire (hugs Jill, rocking her from side to side): Hi, Jill! Ohhhhhh! It's so good to see you!

Jill (hugs her back): Awww! It's good to see you too!

Chris: What brings you to Raccoon, Red?

Claire: Well, Chrissy baby **(she says with a smile)**, if you must know. You see that girl over there? **(She points to Ada).**

And now! Just because I can, surrealism! The camera stops at Chris' head (side view) after Claire says the previous line of dialogue. The format changes to that of 1930's Disney Animation (or Cuphead for you modern NEERDDSS!). We see an animated diagrammatic view of Chris's head, Skull, skin, muscles, eyes, sockets, teeth, but instead of a brain, inside his head, as we zoom in, two eyeballs dance out of a Western bar and then roll out of his 'head' with a hat and a walking stick. They dance to Ragtime Gal! "Hello my honey, hello my baby, hello my ragtime gal, baby my heart's on fire, if you refuse me, honey you lose me, so baby tele, telephone on that dial!" This of course implies that he rolled his eyes so hard at that comment, that they ragtimed out! Heh heh!

Claire: That girl's got some serious beef with Umbrella. Now don't get me wrong, as a journalist, I've seen some serious shit, polluted water, cancer from polluted water, hideous diseases inflicted due to gross mismanagement, nuclear waste, nuclear fallout, political upheaval, attack ships off the shoulder of Orion, etc. The whole deal, but engineering kidnapped citizens to experiment on them and make them into Bioweapons, is something which even the Nazis wouldn't have done. And until I came here, I thought that I'd never believe it.

Chris: No, I'm sure, if the Nazis could, then they would've. I'm sure even we would've. It would've caused a shitstorm –

Claire: Okay, let me stop you there. I need to get her to speak to Leon.

Chris: Okay.

Claire grabs a hold of Ada and takes her to Leon. Claire: Leon, this is Ada. Ada this is Leon.

Lawrence just looks at the two of them.

Leon: Hi, Claire, hi Ada. Claire, it's been a long time.

Claire: Yep. Sorry I couldn't make it earlier. But she wants to talk to someone in charge about Umbrella. Umbrella's behind this.

Leon: Umbrella, the pharmaceutical company?

Claire: Yes, them.

Leon: Well, go to the command tent and speak to the Commander in charge, although, I warn you, he's very busy.

Claire: Yeah well, he'll make time for her, I'm sure of that.

Inside the med tent.

William Birkin walks upto Rebecca and Barry. William: How's she?

Rebecca and Barry look at each other for a moment, but that's enough.

William: She's dead isn't she?

Rebecca and Barry nod.

William (moves towards Sherry and says softly): Let me see her. **Barry and Rebecca continue with their work of helping the doctor. William:** Why is she in chains?

Barry: So that when she turns, she doesn't hurt anyone.

William: My daughter can't.

Rebecca: I understand your love for your daughter-

William: Rebecca, is that your name?

Rebecca: Yes.

William: Rebecca, my daughter is an invalid, because I was an invalid. I injected myself with a dose of the T-Virus, to cure myself. It was a gamble, but I won. I was immune. So's my wife. I gave my daughter an injection to cure her invalidity. It worked. She was able to lead a life of any young child her age. Which is what Annette and I wanted. The T-virus isn't a weapon, it's a cure. It's a bioengineered virus which can cure most diseases, as it was designed as an experimental organic nanobot, which would be far less complicated than designing one from scratch. The Umbrella Corporation designed this as the ultimate cure. A gift, you could say. A gift, you could say with profit motive, but a gift nonetheless. What went wrong was when we accepted a US government proposal to weaponize it for the sake of more profit. Although, I can't blame them either. If someone gave you the ultimate weapon, wouldn't you accept it?

Rebecca keeps quiet, so as to not aggravate him in his time of grief. William: Please uncuff her, I vouch for your safety, as a bioengineer.

And as a father **(he continues softly)**

Rebecca picks up the keys from the table counter and uncuffs Sherry's body. William looks up at her and mouths a 'thank you'. Rebecca just nods.

He then gently lifts her body and carries her out, to the outside.

Outside, as the flaps fall back into place, Lawrence and Leon just look at them in silence.

William heads towards his wife, with their child in his arms. Annette is sitting with Jill and Chris who're trying to provide her comfort through company. As William approaches, Chris shifts to the side, as he sits next to his wife. He places Sherry in

her arms. And they watch her bloodied, but peaceful face. Jill and Chris also look, respectfully. William and Annette don't object.

Annette: She looks so serene, so beautiful.

William: mhmm.

William: I'm glad that she could be happy before she passed away.

Annette: mhmm.

They look at each other and laugh. There's tears in their eyes. Of both sorrow and joy.

Annette: Let's get out of this city. We'll do her last rites at your mother's farm.

William: Okay.

Chris: Annette, there's helicopters here which are evacing citizens out of here. If you want, I can put you, William and Sherry on the next chopper out of here.

Annette (Nods): Yes, that would be very nice, thank you, Chris.

Annette and William show their appreciation for their help by giving them a hug. As they pick up Sherry, and Chris leads them to a helicopter on the nearest helipad.

Claire and Ada walk out, with Claire rubbing the back of her head. Claire: Ow! He threw a file at us!

Ada: At you, you mean.

Jill: Hey! You can talk!

Ada (gives a wry smirk/smile): Humph.

The scene changes to Chris leading Annette and William to a US military helicopter. And helps them get onto it. He steps back, as the helicopter prepares to take off and waves at them, and they wave back, and Chris walks away as they lift off. They look at him, and then look away after some time.

Chris walks back to where the others are. They discuss their next plan of action. This is where my ideas for the start of the movie end. Please take over from here. Mid-movie/End-movie ideas.

How everyone met Private Jonah

Claire and Ada are in search of the military for assistance in evacuation, in this process, they come across an injured woman in military overalls.

Private Jonah (clutching a bandage to the side of her knee): Help me! Please!

Claire (reaching down to assist the desperate woman): What happened? **Private Jonah (through gritted teeth):** I got really badly injured by shrapnel. **Claire (looking at Ada):** Do you have any experience with medicine?

(Ada nods and sits next to her)

Ada (distraught): If I was in a hospital, maybe I could've done something, but out here? With no medical equipment?

Private Jonah: Reach into my bag, I have a first aid kit in there, with some medical equipment. I grabbed what I could.

(Ada searches her backpack, finds a first aid kit and some medical implements) Ada: It's not going to be perfect, but it'll do.

(Ada removes the bandage)

Ada: The good news is that the shrapnel didn't go very deep, the bad news is that infection maybe beginning to set in.

Private Jonah: Then start, please.

(Ada begins working on her) (2 hrs later)

Ada: I've removed it, I've cleaned the wound and the area surrounding it. I've sterilized it. But she's suffered a lot of blood loss. What's your blood type?

Jonah: AB+

Ada: Good, a universal recipient.

(Ada sterilizes a tube with some alcohol and some needles with fire and asks Claire to donate some blood)

Claire: OW! That smarts!

Ada: Just for a second.

(Ada begins the transfusion)

(After a few minutes she closes the transfusion)

Ada: That should be enough for now. Till we get you to a real doctor.

Jonah (a little woozy): You seem pretty real to me.

Ada (looking at Jonah, smiling): How sweet.

(They then pick her up and carry her on their shoulders) Ada: What happened to you?

Private Jonah: I was with my unit, we were assigned to evacuate a block and protect the civilians, when out of nowhere, something attacked us and it wiped out my whole team, except me.

FLASHBACK

Song: Sound The Alarm by Really Slow Motion

0-10: A group of soldiers are seen standing in an urban clearing.

11-24: The Nemesis is seen walking up to a ledge on a rooftop, not very far away (from the vantage point of the sniper), with its weapons bared. The sniper on overwatch for the military outfit is shocked and just about shouts a warning, when.

25-45: The Nemesis opens fire with its minigun. But the marines are able to duck in time. And even though the Minigun fires thousands of high-calibre rounds a minute, the up-armoured Humvees of theirs protects them from the hail of bullets. The ricocheting shrapnel is absorbed by their armour.

46-48: The hail of bullets stop, and as the marines tentatively start to reorganize.

48-1:09: They are suddenly blown to bits by an onslaught of rockets. **1:10-1:11:** As suddenly as it had started, the onslaught stopped. And… **1:12-1:23:** the Nemesis says, "Marines" and then marches off.

1:23-1:34: Samantha, huddled behind an upturned trailer, is the only one to survive.

FLASHBACK ENDS

Claire: Oh my god! That's fucking trash! I mean, that's fucking horrible!

Jonah: Yeah **(grimacing as she shifts weight).** I know.

Claire: What's your name?

Jonah: Samantha Martha. I know, I know, 2 first names. My parents wanted two daughters, so they made me their two daughters. But you can just call me Jonah.

Ada: Well, Jonah, it seems that you got double the love, otherwise how else would you turn into such a fine young lady?

Jonah: Are you flirting with me?

Ada (smiles): Oh no, I would never think of that, I'm just being affectionate.

Jonah (smiles): Yeah.

Claire and Ada, while assisting Jonah come upon a discarded (wheeled) cart and gently out her down on it.

In sometime they come across a bridge, at whose zenith they find a hummer just parked there. They move quickly as they can with Jonah and make it to the Humvee. Behind which they find a group of people. Jill, Barry, Chris and Leon. Claire embraces Chris.

Nemesis Battle Scene (mid-movie scene?)

Song: Storm Is Coming, Junkie XL. Mad Max Fury Road OST. Get ready for 6 minutes and 16 seconds of Badassery.

Booyah, bitches!

0-19: The scene opens with a conked out Humvee (or HMMWV), stranded in the middle of an empty highway. Chris is at another car, looking for spare parts for the HMV. Inside the car, there's Barry, Jill, Claire, Rebecca and an injured US marine (female), a Gunnery Sergeant First Class, Jonah Scott (you can tell her rank by the insignia on her shoulder patch).

20-25: Uhhhh-Ohhhh (in slooww-motiioon), we're fucked. As the Nemesis slowly comes into view (From **Junkie XL's All Guitar Flaming Guy**, take the growling sound effect from 0:14-0:25 and play it as the Nemesis bares its teeth). Rising up from the ground (you know, walking up a slope, geez, I'm not that religious).

25-28: The violin starts to play. This means, shit's about get crazy. Chris' head snaps up as he hears the hollering and screaming from the hummer. As he sees the Nemesis.

28-1:20: 30-48s, Chris runs towards the HMV at full speed, as the Nemesis gets closer and closer. 48-1:04, Chris rushes faster and faster, as the Nemesis' weapons come into view, a stinger missile and a minigun.

Note: The minigun only sounds so diminutive (small, weak, undersized, unassuming, in this case unthreatening), as it is a derivative of the much bigger and far more devastating monster, the Vulcan Gatling Cannon found on Fighter Jets. Designed to incapacitate and damage MBTs (which have 10s of tons of multi-layered, sloped, reactive, ablative, complex and supremely hardened armour on all sides) and utterly destroy light to moderately armoured vehicles. The minigun fires 7.62 mm NATO rounds at 3-6,000rpm from its 6 barrels. The Vulcan fires 20mm rounds (4x the .50 cal anti-personnel sniper round, and 6x the standard NATO ammo) at 300-3,000rpm, from 4 barrels. And the stinger missile platform is designed to shoot down attack helicopters and fighter jets. Attach these weapons to a mutated zombie with high resilience and self-healing capacities, also designed to kill and you're Fucked, with a capital F.

1:04-1:17: Chris reaches the car and tries to start it, many a time (reminiscent of the standoff with the bullet farmer in MMFR). There's now a dead silence in the car, as everyone is waiting with bated breath. The car starts as the Nemesis comes into range.

1:17-1:20: Movement?

1:21-1:33: The Nemesis brings its weapons to bear and it says its catchphrase when it looks at them, **"STARS"** (The Nemesis says the name of its target before it kills them). During the lull in the music (if there's none, you create one, either by lowering the volume of the music, or editing out the music for that duration).

1:34-2:05: 1:34-1:47, the car races away. 1:48, at the pause, the Nemesis fires with its Minigun at the HMV, luckily it's an uparmoured version, and it is able to withstand the incredible beating which it receives, but just barely, one other direct hit from a sustained burst from that thing and they will be Smoked Swiss Cheese (mmmm, just the way the Nemesis likes it). The HMV careens to the right and starts to swerve as it moves out of range of the minigun, to avoid catching even that stray burst. This of course happens from 1:49-2:05.

2:05: And Stop. Stinger time.

2:06-2:22: The Nemesis aims (across the flyover), locks onto the HMV and at the sound of the tone, it fires. The missile streaks across at blinding speed. Chris who's forewarned by Rebecca, when she saw it aiming the rocket launcher at them, knows that there's nowhere to run from it, except overboard (all hands, brace for impact!). And shouts "BRACE!" as he runs the car off the overpass. At that very same moment, Rebecca and Barry quickly squeeze Jonah between their bodies, to protect her from the impact. She grits her teeth in pain, as they're definitely applying pressure on her wound.

2:16-2:18, the car flies (remember Inception, or even National Security?).

2:18-2:22, (at the sound which sounds like an incessant car horn blowing away)the car crashes down on the road (or has crashed down on the road) below.

Luckily, everyone survives, relatively unscathed. As they fell into a massive garbage dump, in a massive garbage truck, and somebody quips, "Thank God for pollution. Thank goodness Captain Planet didn't take pollution down to zero".

Everyone suffers from a terrible concussion, and Jill breaks her right ankle, but other than that, everyone is safe and unharmed.

Side Note: For those wondering where Leon and Lawrence are, they've gone out to the City as an attaché to the military, to look for and rescue as many survivors as possible. This is also where Carlos Oliviera and the rest of the STARS team would come into play. The block in my mind, involves how they all got separated, how they became an attaché to the military, the entrance and introduction of Carlos Oliviera and the rest of the STARS team, and their following adventures. And of course how our present gang came across Jonah, and how she got injured (Jonah encounter, now resolved) Also, let's not forget the Nemesis and how he hounds our protagonists across the movie. Both groups of protagonists, but especially the one Chris and Jill are in, as they witnessed the experiments of Umbrella, in that Godforsaken mansion. That is where the blanks need to be filled in for the story to be complete. And of course, who all die, die, die!

2:23-2:52: 2:24-2:36, they get out of the car slowly and some painfully (especially Jill and Jonah). Luckily Jonah is unharmed. I.e. her wounds did not reopen. **2:37-2:52**, they keep running, as the 'tic-tac' sound in the song matches the pitter-patter of their frenetic footsteps. Jill has a broken ankle and Chris is helping her to run, Jonah is being hurriedly but carefully carried by Barry in his arms, as Rebecca runs beside him, glancing from time to time at their patient's stapled shut, long and deep wound, above where her uterus would be [reminiscent of that squicky scene from 'Prometheus', where the protagonist has the proto-xenomorph foetus cut out of her uterus]. At **2:52-2:53**, Jill, having grit her teeth, quickly resets her ankle bone with a sonorous, loud and sickening CRACK (which echoes across the nearby block (and well within the hearing range of the overpass), as she screams in pain (she's not Deadpool, so there's no wisecracks here, now quick! Read on, before DP punches me in the crotch for this blasphemy!), and this draws the attention of the Nemesis. But, now, she's able to run (she's able to do this magic, because she has enhanced healing from the T-virus as seen in the earlier film).

2:52-3:00: They're all running now ('cept Jonah, of course), full speed towards the military camp.

3:00-3:10: They see the Nemesis off in the distance, and quickly look away, and keep running. But, they hear an Earth-Shattering ***BOOM!***, which clearly alerts them to the fact that that the Nemesis has landed. Shit just got real, real fast.

3:11-3:38: The Nemesis, now having exhausted *his* ammo, throws down the Stinger and the minigun, and starts to run towards them. Each step an Earthquake. Each contact of its foot with the ground, a sickening sound death-crunch and DOOOOM*3. At full sprint, the 8 foot tall behemothenic Death Machine gains at them at an alarming pace.

3:38-4:31: As the Tuba starts to play that heavenly sound of salvation, guess what? Deus Ex Machina. The bright lights of two M1A1 Abrams brightly illuminates their faces. Actually it blinds them (their eyes were stabbed by the flash of a Xenon light, anyone?) (This is reminiscent of that scene from the movie 'Starship Troopers 3: Marauders', where Rico comes to the rescue in his Battlesuit). Something about white light being associated with salvation? I wouldn't know (not to forget the 2 helicopter gunships which also appeared).

Now, the movie becomes something reminiscent (I know that I shouldn't repeat words Ad Nauseam, but, alas, I am doomed to repeat this word, as it is so awesome and infinitely pertinent, apologies, I am a bad writer, and my life has no meaning, boo hoo hoo!) of a silent film. The tanks are so loud, that when one of the infantrymen accompanying them barks out an order to the tanks through his milcomm radio, subtitles pop up, which say, "2- 2! Covering fire! Target 12 O'Clock!" The two Abrams open fire at the Nemesis (for reference of how these particular tanks should sound, please refer to the game Armoured Warfare, especially, their audio upgrade trailer, where you will distinctly hear what 120mm cannons sound like. How punchy, powerful, sonorous and loud their ear-splitting fire-roars are! Ha ha ha ha!) with their 120mm cannons, firing APFSDS (Armour Piercing Fin- Stabilized Discarding Sabot*4) rounds at the Nemesis. The Apache gunships follow up with their own attack with their 20mm cannons, 70mm rockets and hellfire missiles (kinda reminds of the battle scene on the grassy knoll in the 2005 rendition of the 'War of the Worlds', eh?) at the target. They are aware through the advice of CENTCOM that the Tyrants can take a helluva' lot of punishment before they go down for good. The whole group is ushered back, behind the tanks, and into a waiting Bradley IFV (Infantry Fighting Vehicle) (or a waiting Stryker APC, depending on what's more feasible CGI-wise). The group takes shelter, as the Nemesis is ripped to shreds by the overwhelming fire. But then after the heavy pummeling, as it starts to regenerate…

4:31-4:41: In the lull of the fighting, as the smoke clears (preferably in slow-motion, please don't overdo the lens flares), and the infantryman immediately eyes the Nemesis regenerating from the armoured vehicle, he gets on his radio and hollers, "Big Bird, this 2-1 actual, bogey is still active, requesting 1-0h-5 rounds, be advised, danger close, bring the rain!"

"Roger 2-1 actual, this is Big Bird, prepare for lightening and thunder, over and out!"

4:42-5:32: A C-130J Superhercules comes into view [reminiscent of the Skorpinok battle scene in Transformers (2007)] and banks to the left and readies its battery of 105mm (6 rpm) (a motherfucking Howitzer), 50mm (12 rpm) and 20mm (300rpm) rounds, and opens thunderous fire! Raise Hell!

This punishing blow, overwhelms the Nemesis' healing system and renders it an organic soup. Heh heh, ha ha ha!

"2-1 actual, this is Big Bird, we're returning to base for refueling. Stay Frosty. Over and Out!"

"Roger that Big Bird! Over And Out!"

5:23-5:45: What little that remains of the Nemesis coalesces in some strange lovecraftian (any indescribable, nay unimaginable horror) form and it scuttles away (remember The Thing?) forthwith and…

5:46-5:59 and 6:00-6:10: Please put what you like here. Out of ideas for these last two.

Danke Schon.

You'll know when it comes, with warning and without any warning, the Atomic Bomb. Now, we must be ready for a new danger, and this is very, very important.

On an Atomic Melody. The Atomic Bomb. Duck & Cover.

Now it starts.

END SCENE (BAD ENDING) (What follows are two endings, reminiscent of the games)

Music: Papers Please Theme. Lucas Pope.

0-0:45: An F-16 Fighting Falcon (the workhorse of the USAF, then and now) approaches Raccoon City from a great distance. Columns of thick, black smoke are rising from Raccoon City off in the horizon. The pilot goes through all the motions of arming a tactical (nuclear missile bomb). The authorizations, fail safes, etc. The pilot gets a confirmation from command, "Hammerdown protocol authorized" (in subtitles, of course, don't disturb the music now, boys & girls). The initial, slow, pondering start of the music matches the utter bureaucratic and banal nature of firing a nuclear warhead, let's NOT spell this out for audience, 'kay? This is just for you to take note, eh? At the **'0:45'** mark, the pilot launches the missile (1MT). The jet then banks to the right, and then it banks to the left (or 9 O'Clock) and it fires off its flares. As the missile speeds off in the distance as...

0:46-1:19: The music changes tone, and the camera now tracks the missile. On the missile, it's stenciled, 'Sorry'. The camera keeps tracking the missile for this duration of the song, as it closes in on the City, *fast.*

1:20-1:35: The music speeds up. Now is where shit gets real. The missile has reached the boundaries of the City. It has entered the City. It's heading towards the centre of the City, where it will airburst its massive load. It gets closer and closer, as time seems to slow near the **'1:35'** mark. It crosses over a group of zombies as they're inching closer to a mother and her (the mother's holding an M1 Garand aimed at the nearest zombie's centre of mass,

i.e. chest/solar plexus/diaphragm) daughter. They all look up at the direction of the loud, echoing roar of the missile overhead. A humanizing moment. The camera now enters the missile, the nuclear reaction has begun. The Final Countdown. And as the clock

strikes **'1:35'**.

1:35-1:42: KA-BOOM! Massive devastation, as Raccoon City is completely levelled.

The camera zooms out to reveal the devastation inflicted upon Raccoon City, after the music ends. It also shows the many, many US military Black Hawk and Chinook choppers (who're crowding the sky) who've managed to safely evacuate. It's unclear what the hope for the ones who hid in Fallout shelters. 1MT nukes are devastating. The chances of almost all of them surviving 2 weeks are abysmal. But wait a sec, this is weird, the camera seems to be attached to the rear (or at the back of the back) of a helicopter. The camera, our camera zooms out further to reveal a screen, with Wesker standing by it. We see him laugh megalomaniacally at the scene of devastation, and then chuckle, as he turns pensive. As the camera pulls back, we see a long table in what seems to be a conference room, with empty chairs.

The scene fades to black as

The credits roll to 'The Tetris Theme (Dubstep Remix) by Music8Bits. With Hopak (Jumpstyle or Cossack dance as its more commonly known) dancers dancing in Soviet soldier outfits, or just do the easier thing, and seek inspiration or take the footage from the YouTube video, "Soviet Russian Soldier Jumpstyle/Cossack Dance is not a crime!" by lostfanvanjellies22 and interweave it with the credit roll. 'Cept it's now Black and White, with film grain, and it seems like it has suffered from neglect, heat damage and exposure. Nothing too severe, as it still has to be watchable and aesthetically appealing, but it gets the point across of the death, decay and degradation present at the bottom of the neverending pit that is...

RESIDEN

T EVIL HA HA HA HA!

(GOOD ENDING)

Song: Transformers Soundtrack-Arrival To Earth

The group after defeating the Nemesis with the help of the US military and the South Dakota National Guard, drive towards the evacuation zone at the centre of the city, the most easily accessible and defensible part of the city. As the tanks and the AFVs coast along the road, they crest a hill with the rising sun in the background, big and yellow, casting a shadow over the cityscape. They then reach the centre. And the following ensues.

0-47:- They find some tents. As they get closer, the tents give way to large encampments full of hundreds of thousands of people.

Injured, sick, wounded, the poor, the needy, those seeking shelter, amongst them, tens of thousands upon tens of thousands of US military and national guard servicemen and women and police officers offering help and succour to the suffering. And many thousands more civiians, doctors, nurses, paramedics, FEMA, Red Cross, MSF, family members and friends and so on, flitting in-between the many to provide aid and solace. They catch a glimpse of Lawrence, and he of them, as he is helping an old disabled lady out of her wheelchair and onto a stretcher. He is not far from where they are being attended to.

0:48-1:56:- The true sense of the scale of the catastrophe and the operation dawns on them, as they get out of the armoured vehicles and are guided towards assistance by the marines. Jonah is put into a stretcher and attended to. She even finds a comrade whom she thought lost, and cries tears of joy.

Everyone but Barry is tended to for their wounds. As he has none. He marvels at the sight for a moment, and then steps in to help those in need. They are now a part of the mass. The rescue effort. As the camera pulls back to reveal the entirety of the relief camp.

1:57-2:30:- People look up, as they hear the sounds of thousands and thousands of roars. As a mass of helicopters and VTOLs approaches the city and them. Chinooks, Ospreys, Hueys, Black Hawks (amongst one of them, Brad Vickers and Flynn). The sky is darkened, as what appears to be the entirety of the US Military and National Guard's logistics and engineering divisions have come to the rescue of the residents of Raccoon City. Visible even are firefighting, police, news, freight and weather helicopters repurposed as evac and medevac choppers.

2:31-3:06 (Michael Bayhem slow-motion):- The helicopters and VTOLs land with a deafening but awe- inspiring sound. People are orderly and quickly loaded onto the rescue fleet and the rest in the many trucks and armoured vehicles of the Ground Forces. Everyone is either airlifted to safety or taken to safety in the armoured convoy. The planes fill up the sky, and the Ground Force vehicles snake down the roads, which would've lead into Raccoon City in normal times, to exit it once and for all.

3:07-4:07:- Faraway, at an Air Force Forward Base, a military jet, an F-16 Fighting Falcon readies for take-off, as the Taximen salute the pilot. She salutes them back. The aircraft now taxis towards the runway and takes off. The pilot readies herself for the task at hand, as she flies over the Arkley Forest and is on the approach to the city. It is midday now, as the plane reaches the cityscape of Raccoon City and shortly a wonderous sight greets her eyes.

4:08-5:13: One by one, the sky below her is blanketed by helicopters and VTOLs of all shapes and sizes, blocking the view of the forest. The close up shot reveals thousands upon thousands of helicopters. In one of which, the group is safe. The sky clears below her, as thousands of helicopters rush past her. The forest once again visible. She finds the roads full of heavy vehicles thundering down the greyish path, a row of green ants. They're well clear of Raccoon City. Her approach is clear, she readies her missile, fires away, lets lose many flares and bank a hard left heading off back where she came from. The missile speeds towards the City, a streak of white-hot fire. Time slows down as everything becomes quiet.

5:14-5:27: The City now empty except for rats and zombies, it's streets full of paper, it's skies raining wood and smoke, the fierce fires about to be outdone by the incoming conflagration. At the bass note, everything turns white. As the camera pulls back, revealing the enormous explosion and mushroom cloud.

--SILENCE---------------------------------------

INDEX (A)

Major Characters (1968) Sir Edward Ashford (50s-60s) Lord Oswell E. Spencer (37) Dr. James Marcus (50) Brandon Bailey (40-49)

Minor Characters (1968) Ivorian villagers (extras) Ivorian mercenaries (extras) **Major Characters (1998)**

Chris Redfield (25)

Jill Valentine (24)

Barry Burton (38)

Rebecca Chambers (18)

Albert Wesker (32)

Minor Characters (1998)

Claire Redfield (19) Leon .S. Kennedy (21) Joseph Frost (20s) Enrico Marini (20s) Richard Aiken (20s) Kenneth Sullivan (20s) Forest Speyer (20s)

Alpha Team Pilot 1: Brad Vickers (20s) Alpha Team Pilot 2: "Chopper" Flynn (40)*1 Bravo Team Pilot: Kevin Dooley (30s) Edward Dewey (30s)

Girl Mother Father

Leon's Partner

Police and Civilian Extras

Possible Additions [Minor Characters (1998)]

Moira Burton (7) [Seen in picture]

Polly Burton [(3-7) similar to Moira, possibly a bit younger; let's take 5] [seen in picture] Kathy Burton [mid-late 30s (?). Seen in picture]

Lisa Trevor (45). Pale, thin, weak. Torture victim of 31 years. Feral child. Yearns for her mother. Possibly violently insane. Body in extreme disrepair due to decades of biological experimentation.

TEAM BREAKUP (1998)

Alpha Team Bravo Team

Barry Burton 1. Richard Aiken Joseph Frost 2. Rebecca Chambers Chris Redfield 3. Edward Dewey Jill Valentine 4. Enrico Marini Albert Wesker 5. Forest Speyer

Brad Vickers 6. Kenneth .J. Sullivan "Chopper" Flynn 7. Kevin Dooley

1From Battlefield: Bad Company 1 and 2. Just a fun Easter egg. Non-canon.

Organizations/Authorities Major

Umbrella

Raccoon City Police Department

S.T.A.R.S (Special Tactics And Rescue Squad)

Notes

Space will be provided at the end of this document for appreciation, criticism, additions and subtractions (or other things).

All actors and actresses are encouraged to improvise. If the script is lacking, and you can improve upon it, please, feel free to do so. This script is a collection of guidelines. Think of it as an open source project.

Great efforts must be taken in this film as to where editing is concerned, so as to mitigate inconsistencies in this film as much as possible.

For Example:

Bodies that were there in one shot disappear in the next.

In shots taken during daylight, some shadows will appear longer or shorter, showing an unbelievable passage of time between shots.

Or at times the crew and/or the camera will visible on reflective surfaces (such as: door knobs, windows, water, etc…).

We're making an action-horror movie. But that doesn't mean that we have shaky-cam, non- centred shots and madcap editing. We must have appropriately long takes, however long it takes. Steady cam, centred shots, responsible and professional editing.

If you want, we can leave editing mistakes for the lulz.

Disclaimer

This is a work of Sci-Fi, any resemblance to anyone living, dead, (or undead), is purely coincidental. Resident Evil© is a copyright of Capcom®. All rights reserved. 1993-2018. "Chopper" Flynn© is a character from DICE and EA's FPS games: Battlefield: Bad Company and Battlefield: Bad Company 2. DICE EA 1992-2018. This independent production has no affiliation with Capcom or DICE EA.

INDEX B

Credits

Head of art: UA*

Head of cinematography: UA

Scriptwriter(s): Keshav Sapru/open source/UA Director: UA

Assistant scriptwriter(s): UA Assistant director(s): UA Assistant producer(s): UA

Stuntmen/women (if actors/actresses cannot do their own stunts): UA

Stunt Coordinators: UA Cast: UA

Extras: UA

CGI specialists/SFX specialists/composers/costume makers/designers: UA Casting director: UA

*Under Advisement **Budget allocation** Official budget: x Buffer budget: x/2x Total budget: 2x/3x

Possible extra budget source: Kickstarter/Indiegogo. Needed: Greenlight from Capcom.

Distribution

Worldwide. All major video distribution platforms. YouTube, Vimeo, Dailymotion, etc.

Movie length: Short film (10-20 mins), or intermediate (45 mins), or full length (45+), pending on final draft.

Possible special effects engines: Source 2.0 (SDK)

Unity 5 (SDK or paid subscription)

Bullet (Physics engine, open source, free) Blender (free 3D production suite, uses Bullet) Unreal Engine 4 (SDK)

CryEngine 4th Generation (paid subscription) Or whichever one suits the SFX team.

Possible Editing software:

Corel VideoStudio X7 CyberLink PowerDirector 16

Or whichever one suits the editor.

Purchase, torrent or your one. It's up to you, editor.

*SDK stands for Source Development Kit (they're by definition, free)

SCRIPT

The movie opens with the Resident Evil 6 Opening Theme. I leave it to the SFX designers to design the opening (0-10 seconds). 11-12 seconds, the title "Resident Evil" drops. Someone with a deep and menacing voice says the words, "Resident Evil" after the deep bass piano note at 13 seconds. The title stays up for another 12 seconds after which the "Press Start" icon appears underneath the title, it gets "pressed" and it fades to black.

The scene opens in an Ivorian village where Pineapples are grown. We can see a dirt road coming out of a forest into an open field. There's grass on the sides of the road. As we watch, a white jeep and a dark green military truck come roaring out of the forest. They're headed to the village. Just where the village begins, the jeep and the truck stop. Four men step out of the jeep and the soldiers/mercenaries disembark from the truck. The village is completely empty. There's an eerie silence.

Dr. James Marcus: Hopefully, we can find the flower here.

Brandon Bailey: Only a matter of time doctor.

Sir Edward Ashford (turns to the mercenaries and commands them in French): You over there! Clear that field ahead of us!

Lead Soldier (French): Yes, Sir! Move out you lot. Clear the fields! No trouble, do you understand?!

Ivorian Soldiers (In French, Together): Sir, yes sir!

The soldiers move out as ordered. They move through the village. There are signs of habitation everywhere. But there's no one to be found. It's as if everyone left in a hurry. The four men follow behind the soldiers, through the village. The eeriness isn't lost on anyone. As they near the end of the village, there's a small hill walk up. And as they descend, the camera pans out to show a vast field full of red flowers which look like Pineapple flowers. The four men, especially, Dr. Marcus stand agape at the sight. Finding more than they ever dreamed. We can see the entire village in a trance, some rocking back and forth, some humming to themselves, some staring off into the infinite, some curled up, and so on. Men, women and children, all together. They are divided into groups, where each group is entranced in a different position. Some sort of bizarre religious ritual. The soldiers fan out amongst the flowers. And somehow, the villagers at once notice the soldiers and then rush at them with an unnatural speed and with an unnatural scream. Pointing, flailing, gnashing their teeth, etc. The soldiers are taken aback for a moment, never expecting such a welcome. They fire shots in the air, but it does nothing to faze the villagers, they're still running, crazed, at them, like a swarm. The soldiers open up with their AKs. Firing directly into the villagers. Bullets fly everywhere, people die, are wounded, men, women and children cut to pieces. After a number of them are killed, the trance breaks somehow and the villagers scatter, scurrying away from the fury of the fire. The soldiers continue firing intermittently as they herd the villagers into the forest, doing their job. Our group are ecstatic at this sight, they head towards the nearest flowers. Dr. Marcus sits down to examine the flowers. The screams and the gunfire slowly soften, become intermittent and then quieten.

Lord Oswell .E. Spencer (ecstatic): Those barbarians never cared about what was coming at them until we'd thinned the swarm. The virus worked much better than we modelled.

Dr. Marcus (studying a flower, uninterested): Yes, quite. Brandon, what do you think?

(Marcus hands the flower over to Bailey)

(Brandon pours a biological reagent with a base of human hemoglobin and glucose, upon contact, the flower turns purple)

Brandon (pleased): A positive reaction, doctor. It's the "stairway-to-heaven" flower.

Ashford (with relief): Finally! I'd about had it with the bloody Pineapples! Can't wait to get out of this fruity nation!

Dr. Marcus: Bag it and tag it, Brandon.

Brandon: Yes, Doctor!

(The four men call the troops back with the radio. The four men walk up the hill with the flowers In hand, through the abandoned village and then back to the vehicles. They are shortly followed by the shaken and bloody soldiers. Even though the villagers were unarmed, their ferocity is evident. As the Jeep and Truck pull away, we see the Red and Black insignia of the Umbrella Corporation, on the right-handside door of the jeep)

(We cut to nighttime now. At the centre of the screen is a Black Hawk helicopter. Passing swiftly underneath, is the Arklay hardwood forest. Pine trees, Oak trees, Maple trees and so on. We can see the dim outline of the mountains. They are the Arklay Mountains. Inside the helicopter are the members of Bravo Team)

(As the camera moves inside the helicopter. We see, Chris Redfield sitting opposite to Jill Valentine. Sitting adjacent to Redfield, we see Barry Burton. Sitting opposite to Barry is Albert Wesker. Albert is lost in his wristpad, typing away furiously. Barry is lost in thought, with his family's picture in his right hand. He could be staring off into infinity, or looking at his photograph, I leave it to the actor. The photograph contains the picture of his family. Both Moira and Polly are making funny faces in the picture as Kathy is seen playing with the kids. A happy moment. Redfield and Valentine share a smile, a tender moment between the two. Chris then turns to his left and starts playing Andrea Bocelli's "I can't help falling in love with you", on the boom box. Don't worry, this is a parody of predator, but shussshhh, that's just between you and me. Ah, where was I? Yes. Chris starts playing the music and Jill and Chris lock eyes and their smile turns into laughter, Barry chuckles as he puts his photo back into his breast pocket. Wesker doesn't notice, continues typing. Down in the forest, standing on a cliff is the Nemesis Class Tyrant. The helicopter passes overhead with a roar, as it mouths, "STARS". It picks up its heat-seeking launcher, locks on and fires away. The missile hurtles towards the chopper, as the pilots, Flynn and Brad notice the missile warning, change the deployment light from green to red, and deploy flares and

ECMs (Electronic Countermeasures). The helicopter lurches violently from side to side, as the pilot attempts to dodge the missile. The music keeps playing, this adds a surreal and darkly comical atmosphere to the scene. Bravo Team holds on for dear life. Miraculously, the missile locks onto a flare and explodes in mid-air. But not far enough. The explosion rocks the chopper and nearly downs it. Fires break out, and are quickly put out by fire extinguishers. Everyone's shaken. There's damage to the hull, the rudder and the shockwave turned the chopper's windshield into spider webs. They now have to fly by virtual horizon).

Flynn (struggling with the controls and the pedals): Brad! Start the aux hydro pumps. I've lost pedal control, you'll have to take over. Autopilot's dead. Slowing speed, otherwise we'll be done before we even started. The virtual horizon's a bitch.

(Note: Flynn is dressed, casually, not in combat fatigues like everyone else, he just has a military-green aviator's jacket)

(The helicopter slows to a stop and hovers, the light's now green)

Brad (In an urgent voice, makes a clockwise spinning motion with his left hand pointing vertically, while looking back at them): Go! Go! Go!

(The entire team rappels in less than 60 seconds to the ground)

(In the chaos, Wesker runs off into the woods, only Chris is quick enough to notice his disappearance)

Chris (turns violently in the direction that Wesker disappeared): Wesker! Where the hell has Wesker gone to?

Joseph (looking at Chris): Forget him, Chris! We have to look for the Alpha helicopter.

Chris (gesturing forward with the index and middle finger of his right hand, like a gun sign, but with the thumb down): All right! Move out! Sweep the area, it shouldn't be too hard to find a downed helicopter.

(Joseph, Chris, Barry and Jill spread out, searching in the overgrowth. They're on a path leading off into the distance. It's very dark, and only the torches on their guns illuminate the path up ahead. Shortly, they come across the blade of the downed chopper. Joseph, Barry and Jill set up a perimeter around the helicopter, as Chris searches the helicopter, there's nothing in there. But as he crawls out the other exit of the helicopter, which is on its side, he hears a crunching sound, and notices that it's the body of Enrico Marini, he had stepped on its decomposingh and. Only his arm and now broken hand are visible in the torchlight. Chris crawls back and comes out the other end to his team mates)

Chris (addressing them): Nothing. Everybody's Dead.

[At this moment they hear a bark. But it doesn't sound like the bark of any dog they know, it's also very raspy, grating, like as if the throat isn't completely there. It seems to have come from everywhere. Now, the team, while not particularly afraid of dogs, has some inclination about what these could be. They have some idea of what Umbrella has been working on. They don't know that they're building Biologically Organized Weapons (or

BOWs for short, the military loves its' acronyms) for the US military, but they know that gene splicing can lead to favourable mutations, to put it lightly. After all Umbrella owns Raccoon City. Part of the State government's plan to bring "jobs and businesses" to the state.

Apparently, putting the lives of millions in a visibly unscrupulous multi-national biotechnology firm's hands didn't raise any red flags. Now as everybody is on high alert, they are scanning the area around them, the helicopter, they aren't worried about, because it's on its side, so something will have to crawl out of the GROUND to attack them from the behind, but they're keeping a watch on that as well. The four of them have now formed a circular perimeter, a short distance from the helicopter, their torches blazing, cutting through the night, about a metre (~3 feet) or so in front of them. They are all scanning in three dimensions, up- down, left-right, side-to-side, slowly, methodically. They are listening very, very carefully, for nary a snap, or rustle, they are super-attentive, even a cockroach scuttling past would be heard. They reach out with their ears into the dark, through the brushes, trees, into the forest, out 16 metres (~50 feet) waiting then they hear, the feet, so many, all rustling. Then they hear that unnatural growling, barking and snapping. They sound hungry. It's all around them, every direction, they are scanning more aggressively now. Joseph, who's near the helicopter, fires a flare into the air, Jill fires a flare into the brushes, to start a fire to scare off any beasts, Chris, adjacent to her, fires a flare in front of him, Barry who's facing the helicopter, is pointing his automatic shotgun up, to tear anything apart which comes from above the chopper. Now we cut to the view of the dogs. We can see from their FPV (POV) that they are moving rapidly through the brushes, they'll reach them within seconds. This particular dog, is paying no heed to his/her well- being, it's running madly. A branch gouges one eye out, and the dog runs forward as if there was nothing, the only indication that anything happened was the violent jerk to the right, and half the screen going black, as the dog powers through the underbrush. Only the left view is now available. And this is a hazy, grayscale view, as if it's an eye not fully formed, but perfect for the dark. It's probably guided more by smell anyways. The dog jumps out of the underbrush, and for a split second, we see the armored, black silhouette of Joseph, he's prepared, he fires immediately into the dog, the head is blown apart, as other dogs burst through the growth, in the dark, they can't see, but these dogs are half- rotted, their smell is overwhelming. Barry's shotgun, tears a dog to shreds mid- air, as it's still flailing body strikes Jill, on her back. She's startled, but her training keeps her focused, even though she feels the strange sensation of a clearly torn apart Thing still trying to grasp at her with its legs. She shouts, "Run!" As they start to run down the path. Chris hasn't faced any dogs yet. He moves forward, he takes point, then Jill moves out, then Barry, and as Joseph is moving out, a dog tackles him, he struggles, he pulls out his knife, and stabs the dog in the neck, the sounds stop, but the dog doesn't, this is a very surreal sight, a partially silent struggle. Barry takes aim with his shotgun, and shots the dog off Joseph, as a dog attacks him, he punches the dog so hard, that it goes flying off into the distance, he shots the dog, and one shotgun pellet destroys its brain, and it stops moving. In this interval Jill moves to help Joseph up, as Chris provides overwatch (i.e. cover). Another dog bursts out the bush and bites Joseph on his right arm, and starts tearing at it, another dog bursts out and bites him on his groin, this isn't shown in graphic detail, just hinted at, Joseph starts screaming,

and kicking, knocks the groin dog off, and screams, "Run!" Jill freezes for a moment, unsure of what to do, and Barry grabs and pulls her away towards Chris, and they all start running. Just before they're out of earshot, they hear a pin being pulled, and they start running faster, furiously, as they can hear more dogs running after them, and attacking Joseph. There's a huge explosion, as a very powerful grenade goes off (Semtex, High-Explosive). They're almost knocked to the ground from the shockwave, but they regain their balance and keep running down the path in the direction that Chris is running (forward). They're running for their lives as they hear the dogs closing in. parts of dogs, half-mangled, drag themselves towards them, while the ones not dismembered by the blast keep running after them in some capacity. Three-legged horrors, blinded horrors, one or two, four legged, partly dismembered horrors. All this is implied, it's dark, different howls, different sounds, give this away, a few stray flashes from a torchlight, and so on. Anything not incapacitated by the blast is still running after them with great fury and a super-primal drive.

They have a huge head start, but these horrors are running very fast. They are nearing the mansion (the Ashford mansion, "reappropriated" by Umbrella). They can see it. They are rushing towards it, not daring to look back. Chris is bracing himself, gritting his teeth as his breath gets heavier and heavier. As they approach the massive wooden doors of the mansion, he arches forward his left shoulder and braces for impact. He charges forward, all three of them, now in a single line, all bracing for impact. It's beautiful in fact. Years of working together as a team, their bodies and minds are in sync. Chris guesstimates where the lock of the door might be, and fires a few rounds from his pistol, as he's protecting his head, he hears

the BANG! Allows himself a smile, he's emboldened and together they hit the door with such force that it flies open and they all fall face first on the floor. Their eyes are stabbed by the flash of a neon light. No, literally, the entire mansion is lit up. From outside, they were unable to see this, because, A) They were running for their lives and B) Because the windows were darked out. They are blinded by the light. But, Barry is a veteran, he gets up after only a handful of seconds, blinks the strain away, and takes aim with his shotgun. Unlike the common misconception, shotguns have respectable range, if they are designed to do so. He fires, the only surviving dog running towards them, it's decayed features fully visible, its stench overwhelming, its partly rotten tongue hanging out, it's the half-blinded dog, its destroyed right eye hanging by its socket. We have a close up of Barry as he looks very intently at the dog, and as the shotgun fires, we take a second person view of Barry, the gun and the dog, followed by a big boom, as the dog gets gibbed. It explodes into fragments of bone and flesh, a high explosive fragmentation round. There isn't much blood. What little that there is, is coagulated and black in colour. Jill helps Chris up to his feet, and he walks to the doors, and picks up the gun at the threshold. He stops for a moment, as he looks out into the inky blackness of the night, where the trees are moving, without a breeze, he can tell this with the rustling he hears, and the lack of a breeze on his exposed skin on his wrist. He hears the ragged howls of the hellhounds, as he feels a hand on his shoulder, its Barry's. He looks at him, and he looks at him, Barry pats his shoulder, and they both close the doors, drowning out the nightmarish night and its hellish sounds.

They look ahead and they see a huge chandelier lighting up the entire massive room in bright, white, sickly sterile light. There's a massive staircase in the middle, leading up to the top, there's a figure in the middle of the staircase near a body. Rocking back and forth on her butt, she's curled up in a sitting position.]

At this moment, the lights go out. We will take the sounds from the 'The Evil Within, The Assignment DLC" game. When the player presses the start button, there are 2 sounds. At the first second there's a single electronic "bzzt" sound, followed closely by a slightly deeper "bzzt" sound at the second second, and then at the third second, there's a very deep and menacing bass sound which signals the chandelier going out, followed by a barely noticeable 'blowing' sound, as if somebody is blowing out the lights. So, at the first sound, the light directly above their heads goes out, and then at the second sound, the light just a bit ahead goes out, and then the main light goes out at the third sound. And that 'blowing' sound which attracts their attention, as a soft breeze blows through the mansion. Capisce? Good. Everything goes dark, as they hear a shrill scream up ahead, which as you can presume is coming from the figure. As they run up the stairs to the figure. Chris lights a glow stick, as pointing an assault torch at the figure would just destabilize her further. They run up, and they approach the figure cautiously, just in case it's another one of Umbrella's BOWs. They surround her slowly, their weapons holstered. As they come very close to her, they hear her repeating the same sentence over and over again as she's rocking back and forth, now on her haunches, "Losing our minds, losing our minds, losing our minds, losing our minds, losing our minds" in quick succession, ad nauseam. For reference, see the cutscene from the game, 'The Evil Within" where Sebastian Castellanos, the protagonist comes across Leslie Withers for the first time. Chris reaches out and puts his right hand on her left shoulder. Rebecca turns to him and her eyes are red from crying. She has tears streaming down from her face. She's sitting next to a body's legs. It's been mangled. She holds out a patch and gives it to Chris. On it, it says, "Richard Aiken". Jill asks, "What's your name sweetie?" Rebecca responds by pointing to her left breast pocket. It reads, "Rebecca Chambers".

Jill (looking at Barry): Barry? Can you check her for bites or wounds, and see if she has any broken bones of the sort?

Barry: Sure Jill.

Barry gently moves to Rebecca and faces her from the front, with caring eyes and careful hands, he examines her body respectfully.

Barry: Rebecca? That's a really beautiful name. Here. Look at this **(Barry says pulling out and unfolding a photograph from his wallet).** This is my family. That beautiful woman in the middle? That's my wife, Kathy **(Pointing to a laughing woman)**. This here, struggling in her armsthat's my, one of my bundles of joy. That's my naughty Polly, as I call her. She hates that name. That there? With the silly grin and wizened old eyes? That's Moira, my elder daughter. I call her Merlin, she hates that even more.

(Rebecca looks at the photo, looks up to Barry and says)

Rebecca (smiling weakly): That's a really pretty family you have, Barry.

(Before Barry can say anything, Rebecca hugs Barry really tightly and starts sobbing into his shoulder, as if he's not real, and holding onto him for dear life will prevent him from vanishing)

Barry (hugging her back and whispering softly): We're not going anywhere. We're right here with you.

(Rebecca doesn't say anything, she just nods vigourously in his shoulder)

Chris: We should check in with the chopper and exfil her out. Whatever's happening here, we're not prepared for it. We exfil her, come back, get Wesker and get out. Okay?

Jill: Okay

Rebecca (looking up now): Leave, don't stay here, please, you don't know what's here. You don't, you don't, you don't! Leave! Leave now! Please! I'm begging you!

(Rebecca starts to hyperventilate, and starts to enter anaphylactic shock. Barry quickly injects her with an anti-inflammatory, adrenaline and a sedative)

Barry: There's no way to find Wesker, without first getting her out of here safely.

Jill: Agreed.

Chris: Agreed.

(As Barry is stabilizing her, Chris calls in) Chris: Alpha to Overwatch. Come in Overwatch.

Overwatch (Flynn and Vickers in the choppers): Go for Overwatch.

Chris: We have the last surviving member of Bravo team here, we need an evac. How's she doing?

Overwatch (Flynn): Better. We've fixed the rudder, patched the hydraulic piping and the holes in the hull shouldn't matter, they missed the engines. We also replaced the windshield. It's not a hundred percent, but it's enough for the mission.

Chris: That's all I needed to hear. Prep for evac. Alpha out.

Overwatch (Flynn): Roger, Overwatch out.

Chris (looking at his troupe): Well that's it, we better head out, evac will be here any minute.

Barry: Roger, she's stable. Cover me while I carry her.

(Barry carries her in his arms down the stairs. As Chris and Jill cover his front and back, respectively. They reach the doors, and open them tentatively. The dogs are nowhere to be found. If it weren't for the footsteps and the few shell casings dimly visible in the light of the glowstick in Chris's hand, it'd be like nothing happened. Eerie. They hear the roar of the helicopter, as it lands, as Barry lays her in gently. Barry isn't worried since Brad is a medic as well, and so it seems that

Rebecca is as well, judging from her attire and equipment. The helicopter takes off and they head back, closing the doors.)

Barry (Punching his right hand into his left palm): Now let's find that son of a bitch, so that I can pummel some sense into him.

[They move up the stairs tentatively. They sweep right, they sweep left, but nary a fart. Jill finds a doorway on her right. She moves towards the door. And as she moves to open it. We get a FPV view of the door, with everything around it black, as it opens, and we move into a third person cctv view of a dark hallway with the silhouette of Jill visible in the hallway as lightning strikes through a window at the other end of the hallway. We move back to an Over The Shoulder view of Jill. She moves slowly through the hall, with Chris and Barry close behind. She comes across a door to her right, right at the end of the hall (she's moving left, the initial view of her entering the hall was a ceiling view from the right handside pointing downwards). As she nears the door, she hears some moaning and groaning noises coming from the inside. She holds up her right hand and stops them. She says, "sssshhh" very softly while putting a finger to her lips. "Wait at the doorstep. Don't want to startle this guy" Saying this, she turns around, and nearly hits the door with her head, as Barry quickly pulls her gently back by her back strap, to prevent noise. "Thanks" she whispers. And Barry gently nods, as his grim and serious face is weirdly illuminated in the flashing light of the encroaching thunderstorm. The thunder now very audible to say the very least.

Jill gently opens the door, fully expecting a creepy noise, but none comes, as its deathly silent. The room is lit by a warm light from an ornate fireplace at the end of the room. It casts a glow on the whole room, contrasted by the white flashes of lightening and the now booming thunder. If there was ever an ominous foreshadowing this would be it.

She sees a figure, possibly a man by the looks of it, crouched over another man lying on the floor. His head is bobbing up and down, as if he's crying. Jill speaks, but her voice is raspy and dry, like a parched desert.

Jill (Speaking softly, as she slowly approaches the crouched man): Sir?

(Her voice gets drowned by the thunder)

Jill (moving closing, now a POV from her wrist as her hand reaches out to the man, a few feet from her): Sir?

(Now the man takes notice, as his head slowly moves to the left handside. He looks up at her and Jill freezes dead cold. If she wasn't a hardened soldier, she would've pissed her pants by now and would've starting crying for her mommy. There's a rotting face. Grey, soiled, bloody, faeces, sores, flesh in his mouth. And the stench! Oh the stench! He'd not been crying, he'd been feasting on the intestines of the dead man. Uuuuccccckkkkk! Jill feels sick in her stomach. Barry and Chris notice and raise their pistols, but don't fire so as not to hit Jill. The man gets up and starts stepping towards Jill, Jill moves back. Raising her own pistol, she says, "Sir, not one more step, I'll shoot! I'm warning you! Stay back! Sir!" Barry doesn't wait, he shoots the man in the knee, he stumbles to the floor. There's a pregnant pause. Then he starts to get up, shambling forward, using his right leg.

He lurches forward, as Jill shoots him straight through the heart, but to no avail. He grapples her with his raised arms and attempts to bite her, she resists and falls onto Barry and Chris, as they all fall backwards into the hall. The scramble out from beneath her, as the assailant puts his entire weight onto her. Jill bravely resists, but it's much too much, and before Barry can shoot him in the temple. He takes a big bite out of the side of her neck.

"Huuuuucccckkk!" A sickly, gargling sound comes from her mouth, as she gurgles blood out her mouth and blood spurts out of her neck. Barry shoots the monster through his head and attends to Jill. Chris takes out 10 gauzes and presses them firmly, but just enough to stem the flow of blood and not to cause further damage. Barry takes out Morphine, injects her, takes out adrenaline and injects it straight into her heart. He performs a field tracheotomy, so that she can breathe. She grasps Barry's arm very tightly, she's in extreme pain. Far beyond what the human body was designed for. Barry quickly takes out a syringe with a blue fluid in it and injects her in the heart, it's the Antivirus. But it's too late, Jill goes into cardiac arrest. During this time Chris has sanitized two needles with his lighter and attached them to the two ends of a plastic tube, as he transfers blood to Jill, he's a universal donor. Barry hurries with CPR. And directs Chris to use the manual air pumper, which he does so. Barry injects her with the requisite fluids intravenously, and starts to resuscitate her.

Having failed at this, and her pulse steadily dropping, Barry breaks out his field defibrillator, he places the adhesives at the appropriate sides of her chest to depolarize and repolarize her heart. The charge runs through her chest. He does it again, twice, third time, her pulse continues to drop, as Chris furiously keeps pumping air, while frowning intensely at her. 10 minutes later, Barry stops. And with great persuasion, stops Chris.)

Barry (Looking at his watch, speaking into his tape recorder): Time of death. 20:05 hrs. Cause, severe shock caused by a bite to the neck, followed by exsanguination and cardiac arrest. Administered adrenaline, the antivirus, morphine and other necessary fluids. Chris contributed blood. CPR and defibrillation didn't resuscitate Jill.

[Barry and Chris clear up his medical equipment, and throw away his non-reusable supplies. Barry remarks, "Don't suppose that there's a dustbin in this dump, is there?" **He doesn't expect a reply. Barry and Chris after having cleaned up, slump down on the wall. Inside Jill's mind, she's lying on some grass in the middle of a small stream. She's lying on her side, on her side-stomach, so to speak. She's surrounded by water, not much, but it seems like she's on a patch of dry land, an island, the size of her body, dilapidated buildings are all around her. Grassy knolls, a bubbling brook in a nook nearby. A dark expanse behind her in the grassy knoll behind her. She's lying on her right arm, with her left arm trying to cover her eyes from the light. A black dog lightly bounces out of the expanse and hops over to her, a spring in its step(S). As it resolves to the viewers' eyes it turns out to be a zombie dog. It quietly lies down on her left leg. It's lower jaw resting where her upper leg meets her lower leg. The side of the knee. It closes its eyes and lies down there as Edward Artemiev's "Stalker" theme "meditation" starts to play.**

Then! Suddenly! Jill wakes up with a HUGE gasping breath, she sucks in so hard, that her lungs might explode from the strain. Chris and Barry Jump in surprise. They jump so hard, that they are lifted a foot clean off of the ground.)

Chris (as he jumps to Jill): Oh God! Jill! Sweetie! Are you okay! I almost thought that I lost you!

Barry (jumps to gently pull Chris away from Jill): Chris, just give her a little time, she might be in shock or go into one. She's just come back from the dead after **10 minutes (almost not believing**

the words that come out of his mouth as he says them)... Huh. (Looking at Jill): You were almost a Jill sandwich!

Jill lets out an anime laugh (giggle) (It's the one from Phantom Sage and DeTrace's song, PANIC, 1:38-39).

Jill (as she grabs Chris and pulls him in for a passionate kiss): Actually Barry, as strange as it may seem, I feel like I've never felt before! I feel like a million years. Strong and resilient. Muah!

(Looking back at Barry, while her head rests on Chris' right shoulder): Ha! Real funny Barry. (Half-sarcastically, Half-amused, All smiling, perhaps a dashing of laughter?).

Barry (looking at her quizzically): I suppose the T-virus gave you highly regenerative capacity like an axolotl.

Jill (still holding on to Chris): Those are the cute lizards with the sexy fins who can regrow ay lost limbs, right?

Barry: In short, yes? Loosing syllables are we? Let's test for brain damage.

(Barry looks into Jill's eyes, and shines a light, her pupils' don't contract, but then after 30 seconds or so, they start to do so, whatever brain damage there was, the T-Virus healed it. Jill makes a face at Barry while sticking her tongue out.)

Barry: Well, whatever damage there was, it seems that that the T-Virus repaired it.

Jill (breaks away from Chris and slumps against the wall): Well, that's good, isn't it?

(Jill reaches into her pocket, pulls out a roll of tracing paper, tobacco, hash, filter and a lighter. She then proceeds to place the filter in the paper, with the tobacco, the hash and roll them up into a joint. She lights it and starts smoking it)

Jill (looking at them): What? It's not for you, so stop staring. I just had my neck bitten out, so no, you won't get any.

(She continues to smoke, as Chris and Barry just relax, taking a moment, to process everything)

Barry (remarking ruefully): Not that I need anything, promised the missus that I would quit.

Jill (between puffs): That's good.

(Chris alternates between looking at her, then Barry and then lost in his own thoughts. Barry leaps to Jill's throat and rips off the bandage, to reveal that underneath, the wound has nearly healed. There is a lot of gnarly scar tissue all over, especially where the bite took place, but it's mostly closed up now. Barry adds a fresh dressing)

Jill (angry and in pain): What the fuck was that for?

Barry: Had to do it while you were still cranky, and high, so that you'd forget the pain, had to see how fast the T-virus healed you. This regenerative capacity is far, far higher than anything that I've noticed in the world, Natural or otherwise.

Jill: That's interesting. Well, it also explains why people are turning into zombies. Not everyone's genetics are designed for rapid regeneration and mutation. Unlike moi (she says flamboyantly).

(Above Jill's head, a horizontal streak of blood, very, very dim, probably the spray from her violent injury, becomes a darker hue. A nod to the health regenerating from herbs. They all get up and head out the door, but they're surprised that they are not in the staircase area of the mansion anymore, instead the location has changed to a hallway. On the left, is a door, from which some scratchy music is coming, it's Clair De Lune, by Debussy. Chris opens the door and as he enters, he notices an old gramophone playing the song. Next to the Gramophone is a typewriter, also old. He sits down on to the chair, and starts typing out something, as the music fills the room. Jill and Barry sit down on the floor. They close their eyes as they rest. Perhaps they sleep off to go off to some faraway places, eh?

Whatever the director, editor, art director decide for the general scenery and the editing, happens now to set the scene. The camera moves from the left to the right, as it leaves them, it passes through the wall, and enters the hallway, dimly lit, creepy, with lightening flashing through the large window panes. Show what you wish, appropriate according to your feelings. It's beautiful, melancholic, thank you.)

(Chris gets up, takes out the reel of paper and places it on a stack of paper near the typewriter, with a lot of time stamps. Just before he leaves, he notices a metallic emblem of a dog, which seems half complete, and it may fit somewhere, out of interest and instinct, he picks it up and stores it in his right breast pocket. He then moves away from the table and walks towards Jill and Barry and wakes them up. As they head out the door, the music keeps playing, but softer now, as if their actions somehow changed reality. Welcome to reality. They look ahead as the lightening continues to flash. Illuminating the room with light and their ears with sound. Let there be a musical rhyme. As they pass the first Window, the lightning flash breaks out and illuminates their faces with an eerie glow, as the camera cuts to each of the faces, as time seems to s-l-l-l-l-l-o-o-o-o-o-o-w-w-w-w-w-d-d-d-d-o-o-o-o-o-o-o-o-o-w-w-w-w-w-w-w-w-w-w-w-n-n-n-n-n-n-n-n-n. The team can take this opportunity to fill the surroundings with the music of Toccata and Fugue in D minor, preferable from the 4 mins+ mark. In slow motion, and backwards, to make it extra creepy and jarring, as the music slowly starts to rise in volume, intensity and speed, but only for a little bit, as I'm about to start a new scene.

They walk, they keep walking, and when they reach the next window. The music pauses, and time returns to normal, and then Toccata and Fugue starts normally. We'll use the music from the timestamp 0-2:45.

0-20s: As the music starts, there's a sense of ominous undertones. As if something sinister is going to happen. In these 20s, they inch forward, expecting the worst.

The situation taking a toll on their minds. Losing their minds, so to speak (). They're actually aware of this music, as before they start running, they look around, and suspect that someone, probably Wesker, is toying with them, with this music. They don't see the speakers as it's too dark, inbetween the flashes, but they break into a run, so between these two stages of being stationary and then mobile, there's not much of a gap, so it's pretty much a quick, cursory look.

20-35s: As the music rises, they rise with it, and the unnerving surroundings and the past happenings crack their nerves, as they run. The hallway, seemingly endless.

35s-53s: The sound of the music, now matchings their running. As if it anticipates the sound of their foots running, and hitting the floor. Staccato matches staccato.

53s-1:03: As the music reaches its peak, a dog jumps out from behind them. And then the music continues to match their running. Heh heh, as if mocking them for their running. Heh heh.

1:03-1:09: The music matches their running and then from 1:05-1:07, the other dog jumps out from behind them, as they keep running. 1:08-09, At that note, they continue to run, but it also hints at the might of their plight. Running with their tales between their legs.

1:08-1:29: Again, the music matches their running, as they keep running. The dogs come closer, they're very close. One of the dogs comes up near Jill, as she's running, and she hears the dog growl, but what she actually hears is "Panic" which is what the dog says. We'll take this sound effect again from PANIC by DeTrace. At the 2:58 mark of that song. And then she responds with a "It Does Not

Compute" Taken from Media Zealot's parody of this song called "The kryptonian Dubstep Engine" at the 1:52-1:54 mark. But actually I think that it's from the 1964-65 movie, Lost In Space. Anyways, it doesn't really matter. Anyways, she looks forward again and keeps running, as Barry blasts the Dog from the back, taking out its legs and making it fly for a moment in the air, the illusion of it floating there just in mid-air, and then it crashes into the wall a few moments later, with a sickening/satisfying CRUNCH! Its legs blown apart by the force of the shotgun blast, at the best, maybe it has stumps left. And they keep on running down the corridor. Fatigue begins to show on their faces.

1:30-1:33: They are running still, at 1:33, another zombie dog jumps out at them, but it just misses them. And they keep running.

1:37: Another dog jumps out at them. This keeps increasing the tension of the moment. I know it sounds very boring on paper, but that's how it is sometimes. This is also a play on how in Japanese horror (games), corridors are endless.

1:38-1:41: Further running. Sorry, note, with every zombie dog that jumps out at them, they course correct. Wesker is toying with them at this point, he doesn't want them to die at this moment. Zombie dog jumps out at 1:38.

1:44: Another zombie dog. Course correction, further running, music mocks/mimics their running. You get the picture. If you can make this sequence more interesting, please do.

1:44-1:48: Ditto. A zombie dog at 1:48. 1:49: A zombie appears in front of them.

1:50: They stop, surprised. A passage to their left opens. The wall just lifts up into the ceiling, a secret path. If it wasn't obvious, it is now, Wesker is tracking their every move.

1:51: Music mimics their course correction, plus their scurrying.

1:56: The note indicates, a blocked passage, as they have to course correct to the right. Keep right, no left turn. Ha ha, political joke. Anyways, moving on, it's like Benny Hill (Yakety Sax), but the punishment is DEEEAAATH.

1:57-2:11: Further running, the dogs are so close that Barry who's at the rear, has no choice but to empty a whole clip of his auto shotgun into the coming horde. I count 7 zombie dogs. The emptying of the clip, mind you, is of high-explosive fragmentation rounds. One clip has 10 rounds, the dog nearest to Barry explodes in the goriest way possible, 3 rounds gib it. Since it's blind fire, and Barry is just spraying the entire hall behind him with rapid explosive fire, one round, hits the wall on his left, and the splash damage, destroys the front half of the zombie dog near the left wall, the next round, destroys the front of the second dog in the middle, the sixth round destroys the dog nearest to the right wall (from Barry's perspective, all this takes place in the Third Person View or TPV), the seventh, eighth and ninth rounds, incapacitated the three dogs at mid range, Barry's a real good shot. 4 dogs down, 3 to go. The tenth and final round, also incapacitates the dog at long range. And now two dogs are approaching them at long range, one on the left, and one on the right. The tenth round's fragments "injure" the other two dogs and slow them down. An auto shotgun in a closed space with explosive rounds is devastating, as is evident by this masterful display of excellent marksmanship and craftsmanship. Barry, even while blind-firing, took down five dogs in one full burst of his AS. Brilliant.

2:12-2:20: A wall comes down on them as they are about to step through, luckily they escape and unscathed. But they stopped. And the dogs use this opportunity to come into close range. Bummer. But they continue to run, now left. This labyrinthine hall has exhausted them, which was Wesker's idea in the first place. Although Jill is far less tired, as she has awesome power of the T-Virus at her disposal.

2:22-2:26: They see the exit infront of them now. Jill sprints, Chris jogs and Barry looks back aims, and finishes off the last dog with his desert eagle. He moves to reload his shotgun as:

2:27-2:46: They notice a wall coming up from the floor, Jill bounds across and waves them over. Barry reloads both his guns, Chris goes through and Barry follows. They sit against a wall, probably and preferably to their right, as the wall behind them, finishes its closing maneuvre by 2:46.

Barry (spots a camera, on the ceiling, near the opposite wall and gives it two middle fingers as he says): Hey, you motherfucker! Thought that we would die, huh? Well, fuck you, you douchebag, cocksucking maggot whore, wait till we reach you. I'll make you pay. I'll ram my foot so far up your ass that you'll need a plumber to get it out! You fucking whore-mongering bastard. You bloody ou! Ya' blood git! I'll Bury my shotgun uptil the hilt down yer throat ya faggit! Fuck you!

Barry starts jumping like a madman as he stomps the ground in fury and keeps his fingers pointed at the camera.

Jill (as she calms Barry down): Cool it Conan, we can bury plenty of hilts once we find him. Just look over there.

Jill points just ahead of the left wall, to a corridor, at the end of which is a wide open entryway. Time for a big boss fight. Anyways, Chris and Barry look where she's pointing. Chris gets up. They all have their weapons raised and their shoulders scrunched up tightly,

keeping their weapons as close as possible. The regular military offensive posture when approaching a hostile target.

As they're walking, Barry notices a large window to their left, which looks into an operating theatre. Which he can tell, by shining his assault torch into the window. There's a skeleton on an operating table. The only one. It's really creepy. On the door, engraved, it reads,

A.S.R.B. whatever that means.

Barry takes point, while Chris and Jill cover him, as he picks the lock. Barry fails to lockpick and instead attaches a grooved nozzle to his shotgun and jams it between the handle and the door frame. As he's about to shoot, he remembers that he's on auto, slaps his head in self-aware criticism, selects single shot and fires. The lock gets destroyed and he pushes open the door with his right hand.

Inside, he shines the torch at the skeleton, and from his basic anatomy class, he figures out that it's a woman's skeleton.

Barry: That was a woman.

(Jill nods, as Chris just stares blankly. Clearly fatigued by the happenings of the past hour and a half.)

Jill: Hm.

Barry: There's a letter in her hand.

(Barry picks up the letter and asks Chris to read the letter. Chris willingly obliges, anything to get his mind off of the past)

Chris (speaking in a stoic voice): To my lovely daughter, Lisa. Sweetie, it's mommy. I know that you're afraid, the men here promised me that they'll give you this letter. I don't know what's happening dear. But I want you to be brave, they said that I will be able to see you tomorrow, after they carry out the last tests. Don't be afraid, baby, mommy will come to you soon.

Love now and always,

Mommy

(At the end, Chris' voice starts to break, and he stops. Turns to Jill and cries into her shoulder. His psyche is breaking. Jill embraces him and whispers softly, sweet nothings. Barry caresses his back)

Chris (between sobs): You were always the stronger amongst us.

Jill (softly): At least you're not scared of spiders, sweetie.

Chris smiles between sobs, and chuckles.

Jill (cupping his face gently): There, that's the Chris I know. I promise you, no matter what, we'll get out of this.

Chris: I know that we'll never forget.

(Barry gently takes the letter out of Chris' hand, folds it and puts it into his left breast pocket. They walk out, and they hear a soft, "mommy?" Everyone's heart stops. Next to the operating room, there's a cell. They can't see clearly, but as their torches are pointed down, they can make out the silhouette of a person. A very frail person. Then they hear sobbing. Soft, then it increases in intensity and into wailing, interspersed with keening.)

Jill: Oh My God. That's Lisa. Turn off the torches. Chris, turn the glowstick on. Barry, open the door.

(On seeing them, Lisa mysteriously stops crying and turns quite, who knows what she was expecting?)

(Chris turns the glowstick on and Barry opens the jail door open. And the horrific stench assaults their noses so hard that they all immediately vomit. And if it weren't for their military training, they would've probably soiled their pants, with piss and shit. The stench is of rotting shit, piss, flesh, pus and God knows what else. Crusty from decades of rot. They shove alcohol into their noses. To blot out the smells. Jill rushes to Lisa. She's naked and chained to the wall, at her feet and hands. She immediately shoots the chains off. The sound deafens everyone, but Lisa seems to be unfazed, surprisingly, any other feral child would probably have had a far more vicious reaction. Jill moves forward with lightning speed and catches Lisa before she falls to the ground. Barry takes out a warm blanket from his med kit and quickly wraps it around Lisa. Jill in her rage powerfully tears off the handcuffs from Lisa's wrists and ankles. Her super-strength pays off and she feels the deep scars and some blood on Lisa's wrists and ankles. Jill passes Lisa to

Barry gently, as Barry holsters his weapon. Barry takes out the letter from his breast pocket and places it in Lisa's hand. Lisa seems to rouse a little bit from her stupor and smells the letter, as a tear comes down her eye and she mouths mommy. They rush out, closing the door behind them. Lisa is too weak for a sedative and so, they decide that they must take her to the helicopter and make sure that she's cared for. Barry and Chris head off to rendezvous with the Chopper and Jill decides that she will stay back to confront Wesker. Jill gives her weapon to Chris and instead keeps a double-barreled shotgun for CQC. Jill heads left, while B&C head towards the entrance of the mansion. Chris takes point. The camera follows B&C as they head back. The corridor leading straight to the entrance now after all this rearranging business which went on. They reach the entrance, they notice, strangely, that the oak doors of the entrance are locked again. Chris remembers that he has the dog emblem in his pocket. He takes out of his pocket and fits it into the incomplete dog emblem in the centre of the door, where the lock is. It makes a click sound, as it fits perfectly. He turns it left, turns it right and then turns it right. A very simple puzzle, which somehow comes instinctually to him. The door opens with a very satisfying and deep CLICK as the doors slowly open inwards. They head out into the night. As Chris keeps a look out for the dogs. Lisa has comfortable fallen asleep in Barry's hands. Like a baby.)

Chris: Overwatch, this is alpha, come in, over.

Overwatch: This is Overwatch. Reading you loud and clear. SitRep.

Chris: Request evac. We have another survivor to rescue. Not from Bravo, she's a civ.

Overwatch: Roger, Overwatch incoming. **Chris:** Roger, awaiting. Over and Out. **(Chris looks over to Barry and Lisa)**

Barry (Looks to Lisa, who's in his arms): Just a little longer, okay?

(The scene cuts and we move over to Jill. Jill moves towards the doorway, and instead realizes that hidden in the darkness, there's a very long, winding staircase, leading down to a basement. She has her pistol drawn, and her assault torch lighting up the dark, as much as possible. She goes down the winding staircase. As she enters Umbrella's underground library, I.e., Wesker's Laboratory, its pitch black. Before reaching the end of the staircase, she switches her torch off. She can't see anything, nor can she see anything. Even with her enhanced sight, smell and hearing, due to the T-Virus running through her veins, she can't sense anything. Not a cockroach, not a fly, mosquito, rat, mouse, cricket, nothing.

She walks, slowly, very slowly.

Her gun raised, she tries to scan the room, while reaching out with her enhanced senses for anything even remotely hostile. Nothing. Then she notices tinnitus. A ringing in her ears, with no apparent source. It gets louder and louder, louder and louder, till the high-pitched ringing is deafening. Till there's a sharp pain in her head. Still, it doesn't stop. She falls to the ground, holding her head and screaming, at the top of her lungs. Even then, nothing penetrates the intense ringing. It takes her to the edge of sanity, where she can stare down at the precipice of madness. A void, ready to engulf her. Suddenly, she feels a force, reach around her arms and gently pull her up, and make her stand. She can't resist, because of the pain. Then, through the pain, she feels the warm and electric sting of a needle, and she freezes completely and the ringing stops.

Albert Wesker derives a sexual thrill by trapping his prey. An unparalleled sexual desire.

He runs his index finger up and down her spine. She feels his finger on her spine and is petrified. She's afraid, but can't do anything.

Only her eyes can move, and all she can do is glance back. It's still dark, but she is able to make out a faint movement behind her. The silhouette of a man.

We can depict the characters in the dark as well. For the idea of this form of representation, please refer to the dark level in Hellblade: Senua's Sacrifice. For the convenience of the audience, of course, she still can't see. But Wesker can, his senses are more sensitive, and more attuned.

He speaks. It's an icy, unfeeling voice, tinged with sexual arousal.

It's like the buzzing of a fly. Inhuman. Yet somehow the words roll off of his tongue in a language that humans can understand.

"Jill. What a pleasure it is to have you all to myself. I'm going to do you a favour. We're going to fight, but for that, I needed to scare you. You're frozen, this is a high dosage of Strychnine. The T-Virus will remove its effects in a few minutes. In a few minutes, you will start recovering your senses. But, before that, I'm going to break your goddamn spine.

Punch through your stomach (Wesker makes a fist and touches her lower back, a taste of what is to come), of course. This will hopefully not kill, but instead, the T-Virus will sense and overwhelming danger to which it can't counter, and will immensely enhance your response times, that, or it will kill you dead".

With that, Wesker punches his hand through her stomach. His open hand. Just to show off how much strength he has, and to cause as much damage as possible.

Her front explodes into tiny shards which blast outwards. If the pain from the dog bite was a one, this would be a 100. This is far, far beyond what any normal human could withstand. A normal human would be dead in milliseconds. So, the effect is not unlike that of a shotgun blast, with the barrel pressed against your body. Devastating. We don't really see it, as much as we hear it. His hand hits with such force, that even the armour is incapable of stopping it. He revels in the gore for a moment, turning his arm in what remains of her lower torso, and then pulls his hand out. Wesker licks her face. He tastes something warm and salty trickling down her cheeks, it's tears. And he says (like pinhead, but a bit more human and soothing, still menacing though, and that's saying something), "Oh, no tears please, it's such a waste of good suffering!"

Wesker wipes her tears away, and moves behind her again. And then places his hands on her shoulders.

The T-Virus, sensing an indomitable force, goes into hyperdrive. Evolution and repair goes at trillions of times the normal rate. It is of course, excruciating. No wonder most people turn into zombies or go violently insane.

She starts breathing very fast, her fat, oxygen, salt and sugar levels drop precipitously. Her heart rate crosses 250 bpm and her blood pressure threatens to destroy her circulatory system.

After her body heals. The effect of the strychnine wears off, and she feels very weak. Albert, now surgically injects her with a ultra-dense serum which provides her with all the energy and nutrients, plus adrenaline which she would need.

She takes a deep breath as her energy returns manifold. She can feel her muscles tightening, her belly fattening, as her energy levels move to reserves.

The transformation is sudden and shocking.

"Now, you are ready", He says.

He claps his hands in a thunderous manner. A sonic boom reverberates through the lab. As super-bright-white lights come on, and even though she is blinded and deafened, she moves back, as if she's gliding in the air (slow-motion?), anticipating an attack. It's surreal, graceful and beautiful. Her eyes are open now as she glares at Wesker.

She is thus able to dodge his opening attack.

While I will not break this song down into its nitty-gritties too much. I will give the basic gist (outline) of the battle. The director, editor and stunt choreographer can take it from there.

Every blow is a sonic boom or a thunderclap. The lights go out with the sonic booms. It's dark again. There isn't much energy in a sonic boom, but it deafens Jill every single time (which we can simulate with a high-pitched ringing and pain.

Eventually, due to the presence of the T-Virus, Jill goes deaf no longer) and causes all the glass in the room to shatter. Albeit, the shockwaves generated from the impacts of their attacks and blows meeting, destroys anything which isn't reinforced. For these 4-5 minutes that they are fighting, it's a very close up, furious, visceral and brutal fight. The song which they're fighting to is "Die,

Volter!" From the Killing Floor 2 soundtrack. Perfect for a boss battle like this.

1:33-1:45: There's a lull, I leave it to the rest of the crew to decide what it is that they wish to do in this lull.

1:53-1:56+: The rapid fire (3) staccato beats which sound like automatic gunfire. Jill is firing at Wesker with her auto assault pistol. He dodges the bullets at near point blank range. And disarms her, as they're locked in a deadly embrace. Jill breaks away, and they continue to fight. Using whatever they can find. Guns, germs and steel. Rip and Tear, Motherfucker!

2:34-2:47: There's a lull in the music. There's also a lull in their fighting. Both are tired and badly hurt from their respective vicious beatings which they've inflicted on each other, neither wants to give. This is inspite of their hyperactive healing.

They look at each other, Jill smiles a sort of menacing but appreciative smile, because she has a worthy opponent. Wesker returns the smile but for unknown reasons, I leave it to the actor.

2:54-3:02: Jill had moved to attack Wesker, but he had disappeared with blinding speed. At 2:54, when the harsh violin note plays, Jill notices out of the corner of her eye (right eye? Her eyes are now accustomed to the dark, the T-Virus compensated), when she's still on her left knee, that Wesker is coming in with a harsh and swift blow, it hits her. And when the mellower violin note plays at 3:01- 02, she shrugs off the blow to her face with a shrug (this is played for comic effect).

3:30-3:56: The fight starts to wind down as they are both exhausted beyond belief (i.e tired).

Of course throughout all these sequences, the actors shouldn't forget to make noises in response to blows or running, etc. etc. I mean, after all it isn't two plastic bots scraping against each other, it's two humans beaten the living shit out of each other. Make more hateful love than even metal robots, you bloody ouhs, what the ouh are you doing? Blindness! Sound! Action!

3:56-4:08: A brief lull, please fill in the blank(s) as deemed appropriate.

4:09-4:12: The brief rising violin theme. Wesker leaves quickly. Jill is now loses consciousness as the injected neurotoxin takes effect. Argh that simy bastard, he slipped in this nuclear roofie when he was injecting the strychnine, it must've been primed for time! Arrghh! The bastard! El Bastardo!

DOOM (2016 OST)

-Message from Dr. Samuel Hayden/Title Drop 0-38: 6-8s, 13-14s, 19-21s, 26-27s.

The heartbeat sound signifies that Jill is still alive as the camera creeps ever so slowly towards to her. Interspersed by big jumps in the gaps between the heartbeats, almost as if the camera is afraid to approach her heart is aware (i.e. beating. Muah ha ha ha!).

28-30s: At the "dhun" (i.e. bass drop or BD) sound, Jill's eyes open as the camera is close to her face, not too close. About a half-foot (0.15m) or a foot away (0.3m).

33-38s: Jill gets up, is dazed, disoriented and looks around. We can perhaps take inspiration from the MMFR scene where Max gets up after the sandstorm and experiences a hot flash (flush?). Inspiration of course, create something to match the music at this point, with the camera and the editing, of course. Oh well, or do what you please. These are of course, suggestions.

We stop the music after this timestamp.

Everything is silent. A silent as when she first entered the lab. And the lights are still off, because the lights broke during the dark.

Red emergency lights start flashing. This disorients her further. She feels fear, a tightness in her chest. She holds her chest and takes off the mangled armour she's been wearing all this while. She unbuttons the first two, three buttons of her shirt (black, part of her combat fatigues), so that she can breathe. She takes deep breaths.

-At DOOM's Gate, Extended Version by ArcheoN

0-3, 6-9s: The theme starts to play. The deep bass sounds represent (inception fog horn), the siren alarm, as the red emergency lights strobe. Jill is not deafened anymore, but the alarms do cause her great discomfort, as she puts her fingers in her ears. While the alarms play, two giant stasis pods open. One in front of Jill, and one at back, her back. As two massive, naked tyrants (with smooth crotches, no genitals, like AOTitan) step down. They are grey humanoid males. Sort of like AOT, but much smaller (but still huge compared to iddly-piddly, teeny-weeny, tiny-winy, ok, I'll stop now, humans, sorry, can't help myself). Even so, they're huge, extremely muscular, and they look as if they could survive hits from 20mm rounds, easily [I.e, twice the size of personnel destroying rounds (50-cal), or WW2 anti-materiel or anti-tank rounds]. They are hairless (so ugly). For reference, please look at the tyrant in the Resident Evil animated film, "Resident Evil Damnation (2012)".

They are 10 feet tall and 8 feet broad. They are ginormous.

0:11-0:23: Their de-stasis continues as they stretch their neck muscles and shrug off the stiffness and open and close their fingers. Crack their knuckles, and do jumping jacks (or star jumps), the ground shakes, as Jill rocks back and forth on her haunches, as she tries to regain her balance, while slightly puzzled and bemused by something so menacing acting out something so harmless and childlike, it's funny, because they do it with completely straight faces (you could make them gay, but I leave that to you). Jill gets up quickly and looks ready to run. The camera pulls away into the distance to see them from afar.

At 24s, as the first pair of staccato BBs (Bass Beats), the camera cuts in ("dhun- dhun"). Each beat in quick succession. The first "dhun", the camera moves halfway to Jill, then at the second beat, we move into Jill's first-person view.

At 25s, the second pair of staccato BBs, the camera cuts to her view of the exit, to her left (the first "dhun"). At the second "dhun", it cuts to the wide-view. The tyrants are slowly moving towards her (this is slo-mo). She's not very far from the exit, but neither are the tyrants.

At 30s, the third pair of staccato BBs, with two "dhuns", she notices each of the tyrants (one per beat). She's already running.

At 31s, the fourth pair of SBBs, we switch to the FPV of the Tyrant on the right of Jill, with the first beat. With the second beat we zoom in on Jill from the right tyrant's POV. Continue whatever action already underway.

At 36s, the fifth pair of SBBs, we switch to the FPV of the Tyrant on the left of Jill (trained at Jill), with the first beat, with the second beat, the view of the Exit.

At 37s, the seventh set of SBBs, we cut to the right tyrant's FPV (POV), with the first beat, that of Jill, and then with the second beat, the POV of the exit.

At 39s, the eighth set of staccato beats, we cut to Jill's face, her desperate expression (with the first beat), then her POV of the exit (with the second beat).

At 40s, the ninth set of staccato beats, we've achieved a climax. We cut to the wide view with the first beat, and with the second beat, we cut to the medium view, centred on Jill. We can see her run, and the determined looks of the Tyrant's trained on her with laser focus (even if they come off as determined, this is barely noticeable, a, due to the low light and b, because they're basically machines, they don't have much expression at all, really).

41s-1:02m: We're out of slo-mo, Jill runs for her life. The Tyrants run for her, she barely makes it. The Tyrants' grabs barely miss her by a hair's breadth. Phew! A close call. Didn't want to kill off one of the leads so soon.

1:02-1:05m: As Jill reaches the exit, those 3s of quick beats (4 pairs), zoom into her shocked face in bursts (crash zoom?). Her mouth's open, her eyes wide, as the Tyrants loom ominously behind her.

1:07-1:18m: She's back at the corridor which leads to the mansion exit, the place changed shape again, and she didn't have to climb up the stairs [as is common in games (especially horror games) and in Jap/K Horror]. There's also a whole bunch of zombies in front of her. From regular zombies, to dog zombies, Lickers (please refer to the resident evil wiki) and creepily, eerily and impossibly enough, zombies crawling, jumping, slithering and basically fucking out of the ground. It's as if they watched the American Martin Mystery Cartoon (the boogeyman episode). Boy, this should really fuck with the viewers' minds. Not to mention, they also teleport into existence like COD zombies. Ha ha ha, ha ha ha, HA HA HA!

We then, keeping with the Video game theme, we see time slow down, and the surroundings (except for Jill) blur out, as the weapon hot-switch menu from DOOM (2016) comes up and "Jill" scrolls to the super-shotgun (sawed off double barreled shotgun), selects it, and let the mayhem begin! We go back to the normal view. And we see Jill from a right-handside, medium distance, with the supershotty in her hand (ready to blast any freaks away). She's right handed, right index finger on the trigger. Left hand on the barrel.

She's ready to fight.

At 1:19m, 1:20m, 1:25m, 1:26m, 1:31m, 1:32m, 1:34m and 1:35m: the eight pairs of staccato beats. For this entire sequence, Jill fires her shotgun. The first beat of every pair, shows the shotgun blast (fire), from a 2-D sidescroller view, then the second beat, shows the result, gibbed zombies at point blank range with the fire of the blast of the shotgun with hot shrapnel, shrouding their bodies. This way, she dispatches 6-12 zombies nearest to her. Some of them are close to her, some far, some grouped, some spread out, I leave the final shotgun massacre count to you. She fires 8 times. 8 beats = 8 shots. At the 2 five second intervals, I leave upto the director as to what to do. She's running forward as she's doing this. The Tyrants are close behind, always one arm's length away from her. She's too quick, they're too bulky.

1:37-1:57m: Jill, after running out of ammo. Goes all DoomGuy (or DoomGal) (or commando) on their ass. She glory kills everyone of them. Hand through face, face through hand, snapped neck, punched through the heart (dhukkh, dhukkh, SPLOTCH! As she crushes the heart in her hand, or jams it down the zombie's throat), torn apart, dismembered (literally and figuratively, including their members, if they have one), eviscerated, gibbed by her jumping through

their bodies like Bo Rai Cho's brutality in MKX, etc.

While doing this she's looks furiously determined, but also has a maniacal grin. Ear to ear.

She's moving down the corridor to the mansion doors which lead to the outside (they are open).

1:57-2m: She reaches the mansion doors, at the four sets of staccato beats, the camera zooms in on her (in bursts, crash zoom), as she bursts out, looks at the sky and smiles. Cheer up love, the cavalry's here. It's also dawn now, turns out, she was knocked out for quite sometime. Even the T-Virus takes time to undo the effects of a neurotoxin. The sky has that slight bluish twinge to it.

2:00-2:02m: She runs a little further, inbetween the row of trees, in front of the mansion. A small open space, and the helicopter with Flynn and Vickers at the helm is there.

2:02-2:13m: Jill waves at them with her left hand to her right. And then shows them a two, to signify meeting her two clicks (2 kms) east. They'll make it there quick. As the Tyrants follow her. She also gestures to them to go full throttle (a fist up) and danger close fire (her right finger stabbing her open horizontal left palm with great force and immediacy). She's running there while doing this. She gets a thumb's up from both Flynn and Vickers.

At 2:14m: The first pair staccato beats, we crash zoom into Brad Vickers pointing from his heart to the Tyrants with his right hand. Like the People Eater did towards the end of MMFR, when he pointed at Mad Max.

At 2:15: The second set of staccato beats, we crash zoom to Flynn giving the Tyrants the middle finger.

2:15-2:20: Interval, please fill as necessary.

2:20m, 2:21m, 2:26m, 2:27m, 2:29m, 2:30m, 2:31m and 2:33-2:52m: The Black

Hawk Gunship fires its rockets at the Tyrants [A BH gunship has 2 rocket pods for a total of 72 rockets, 2 Gatling cannons (super-rapid, super-heavy machine guns, 20mm rounds with 6,000 rpm rate of fire, 6 barrels each. Ours has 3, one at the nose, in front of the cockpit) and 8 hellfire missiles]. The first beat of every set, shows the rockets firing, the second beat shows the explosions. In these 7 pairs of beats, the gunship empties its entire load onto the Tyrants. (From 2:33-2:52m) It's also firing its Gatling cannons (in short and quick bursts, as they have very heavy recoil, and could end up making the helicopter fly backwards eventually).

The helicopter bucks, strains and moves backward to some extent as a result of the heavy firing. The tyrants do stumble, fall and recoil heavily from the battering they received. There are many small and medium wounds on them, but they're very tough. Having softened them, the high calibre ammo makes them dodge and weave as they chase after Jill, but their regenerative capacities, allow them to pursue her. The internal damage must be intense, and one of them got blinded.

Healing takes time, all of this action prevents them from catching her. They are very tough. As the music starts to reach its crescendo, the helicopter reaches the rendezvous point, and drops its height sufficiently, that she with her intense super-strength can jump straight in, just before the Tyrants get her. A 1-2 metres away (a few feet, midget to average human length).

2:52-2:55: With the last 4 sets of super-staccato beats, the helicopter crash- zooms away.

Then, behind them, the mansion blows up in a huge thermobaric explosion (not thermonuclear). The helicopter is quite faraway now, so the explosion rocks the helicopter and causes a small fire to break out, which Chris immediately extinguishes, as he's nearest to it.

Flynn (Laughing mockingly with some frustrated mirth): Gotta hand it to ya zombie, ya got no quit in ya! Ha ha!

Vickers: Thanks, Chris.

Chris nods. Lisa is on the floor of the helicopter with Rebecca sitting next to her. She's cleaning her body gently with wet wipes, with a blanket covering her.

There's various intravenous fluids going into her, blood, glucose, saline, etc. And bandages covering her where needed.

Barry (Speaking into his tape recorder): Remaining survivors all accounted for. Jill and Chris rescued. Lisa stabilized, Rebecca is helping to take care of our patient. We're enroute to Raccoon City to get proper medical assistance. Unclear as to what the future of STARS and the Umbrella Corporation will be, perhaps, this will make the government wake up and take action, finally.

Chris and Jill just silently watch him, and each other, sharing a look of affectionate concern and exhaustion. As they all silently sit and take in the moment, the camera moves out of the helicopter through the door and then it pans away to show the whole helicopter, the dawn (as the sky starts to lighten up, must be around 6:30, it's summer, so dawn comes fast), and the faint glow of an explosion in the background. Far off in the distance, Raccoon City is visible.

The scenery shifts swiftly from the helicopter, points downwards to the jungle and moves us through it [with much rustling and cracking, and the various sounds of the Jungle, as if we ourselves are moving through the forest (i.e the camera/audience) at great speeds] to that of a city (passing over a river with a bridge), and then swiftly (accompanied by all the familiar sounds of a city) from there through the city to inside the compound of a reasonably well-sized suburban home. Behind large steel gates, a girl is playing hop-scotch. The camera tracks her back, zooming in more and more slowly. Till she faces forward again, to complete her next round. Moving her fingers in front of her, like the girl from the music video of Skrillex's song, First of the Year (Equinox).

-Skrillex – First of the Year (Equinox) (original mix)

0-36s: As the music starts playing. The little girl starts her hop scotch back. Still playing with her fingers, lost in her world. Her mother is watching her from the kitchen, as she's arranging her groceries. As she ends her jump back, near her gate, right in front of her (side-view), she looks up (a quizzical look).

36-39s: As we cut to her mother rushing out with a knife in her hands.

40-52s: Seeing this, her father runs down the corridor (hall) towards the door which exits their house. We see a sports match playing on the TV, as we hear crowds cheering, in-sync with the music around the 44-52s timestamp. This is, of course, for thematic effect. He runs out, and as he's coming to see his daughter on the floor dying, the camera closes on his face in jerky manner (like as if someone is turning time back and forward very quickly for short intervals of time, or you could think of the temporal equivalent of when DJs create that distortion effect with their turntables, by turning their gramophone like discs backward and forward, or like how similar to how it happens in the music video of the song), it alternates between him slowing down as he comes to a halt, and the sight of his badly injured daughter and the sight of his partner cradling their daughter on the floor, as a man off in the distance is lying on the road with a knife in his head, a bite having been taken out from the left-handside of her neck. This quick alternating matches the frenetic pace of the song as it reaches its peak, this is happening in slo-mo, and as the beat rises from 0:53 to 1:04 (we Dolly Zoom to his face). This is to express shocked surprise (Jaws, anyone?).

1:05-1:07: In sync with the song, the camera cuts to the mother suddenly, as she looks up at him from his POV and shouts with her eyes closed, "CALL 911 NOW!"

Hopefully, this doesn't fall into the trope trap of showing men as useless.

1:08-2:00: The scene quickly cuts to an extreme close up of the strobing lights of a cop car (patrol car), the camera tracks its frenetic movement, while it's focused on the lights. It's speeding through the streets of Raccoon City. Cutting past heavy traffic jams all over the city (hinting at something rather sinister and ominous).

The cop car mounts the curb(s) (it doesn't run over anybody, duh, theese izz natt GTA, Komrade). Just as we approach the two minute mark, everything goes into slo-mo again, as the car turns into a mass of panicked and running people (who're running away from them).

2:00-2:12: At 2:00, in sync with the song, where the sound of the crowd cheering is heard, the car in this duration slowly moves through the crowd, gently, so as to not hurt anyone, as people rush by (in slo-mo). The police officer driving the car, and his partner, quietly take in the strange sight. The left breast pocket of the driver reads, 'Leon .S. Kennedy'. The car approaches a police barricade, and at 2:12, as the line "Radio-Start" begins, they get out. Time returns to normal, but I'm not sure.

2:13-2:24m: So, with the line, "Radio-Start" they get out, and look at the crowd. They see things which terrify them, as Leon begins to call in for backup. He raises his weapon, as does his partner (a black man), and they get ready to protect the crowd and fight whatever menace they can (perhaps there are fire engines, ambulances and other patrol vehicles around. I like to think so. That where they stop, there's a police barricade on the road. And one or two SWAT trucks too. But strangely enough no other cops are around, or any other member from emergency services. Busy or otherwise). With this, the music quickly rises, as the camera quickly pulls away from them, through the streets, blocks, upto a satellite view of the city, then the world, as...

2:25-2:26: The screen fills up with people (on their phones, or otherwise) shouting, "Call 911 now!"

HA HA HA HA! THE ZOMBIE APOCALYPSE HAS BEGUN!

2:27-4:21: The credits roll. I'll leave it unto you, whether you wish to have a generic credit roll, or something stylistic and artistic, matching the frenetic pace of the music? A skull perhaps, white, but not too realistic, distorted, matching the surreal sensibilities of this whole setup. In the background in the front, or wherever.

If the credits don't finish, we can play the Battlefield 3 theme song. Post – Credits Scene

After the credits roll. The post-credits scene takes place. It opens up with the whole cast of Resident Evil standing in a 'V' formation, facing us. Hopefully, the BF3 theme might still be playing (although at a much lower volume).

They're all looking badass, with all of their own looks.

If you want to make it like COD with all the emojis at the end of MP matches, by my guest (NOT).

Anyways, Jill is standing in the centre of this formation, and the camera focuses in on her, as she's standing either on her left side facing us, or full frontal. She says looking proud and intimidating (i.e. badass), and she says (weapon in

hand?), "Resident Evil has changed" And then the camera crash zooms to her left eye (extreme close up, eye fills frame), and she continues (in a softer and calmer tone), "Are you ready?"

For inspiration, you can watch the ending of the trailer of the video game, "Borderlands 2"

-CUT TO BLACK-

-END TRANSMISSION-

SEX IN INDIA

The scene opens with a couple getting married. They are coming together. As they move in to kiss, flowers and garlands of flowers close in like curtains in a play, obscuring them. A euphemism for sex. The act of climax is represented by hundreds of flowers flying into the air, thrown by people.

The birth of their child is represented by a baby flying out from a pond into their hands. Waterbreaking and birthing all represented (depicted) in one go.

Oy Vey!!

:D

SUPERMAN

Song: Superman theme * John Williams

1: 0-1:13, 2: 1:14-1:42, 3: 1:43-2:03, 4: 2:04-2:20, 5: 2:21-2:56, 6: 2:57-3:17, 7: 3:18-

3:53, 8: 3:54-4:02, 9: 4:03-4:07, 10: 4:08-4:20, 11: 4:21-4:22.

1. The scene opens as Jor-El on Krypton places his young son into the rocketship to blast off to Earth. As he speaks in Kryptonian, the subtitles read: "Take our hope and give it to a World under a new Sun". Saying this, Jor-El places the blanket with the Superman logo (Kryptonian for hope) on little Kal-El. As he steps back to his wife. Then the rocket lifts off and blasts off into space (we show Krypton in the background, but we don't show it explode as the spaceship blasts off to Earth (there's a faint glow in the background, people can interpret it for his cousin's ship or Krypton exploding).
2. The ship is seen passing by Jupiter as it nears Earth. Then it flies through the sky in Kansas, as Martha and Jonathan Kent in their '50s pickup see the ship fly through the sky, above their ranch. They come across the baby Kal-El.
3. Kal-El tests his powers as he runs by a train at super-speed, his clothes catching on fire, due to the friction created by the rapid movement. The people in the train gawk at him, as they see a human torch running past their windows. He then jumps far down into a creek between two cliffs, to put out the fire (as the skies darken), as the train passes over a bridge. We see him underwater, and then he rises out of the water, his clothes in tatters.

There's a tornado rolling across the Kansas countryside in the distance, as he blasts off with super-speed towards it.

4. The residents of Kent who were running underground from an F-5 are left gobsmacked as they stare with their mouths open at the sight of a half-naked man floating in the sky, stopping a tornado with his breadth, as the winds whip their bodies and houses, it's a most awe-inspiring sight. We see Superman's face as he's putting in immense effort in trying to match the force of the tornado (He succeeds, obviously, there's no critical failure here).
5. Mild-Mannered Clark Kent is sitting at his desk working on an article with the title, "SUPERMAN STOPS TORNADO!" (Not in New York, he's not there yet). He saves a little girl's kitten (and puppy) from a tree (as a normal human), as he sets off in a train for New York, after saying goodbye to his parents. While at the Daily Planet, working, he feels the building shake as an Earthquake dislodges the Daily Planet globe and sends it hurtling down. He tears open the shirt (as the music rises) to show the 'S' symbol underneath.
6. He stops it from hurting anyone down below! And then he hears something from his super-hearing and blasts off into the air.
7. He flies to the Soviet Union (Ukraine SSR), to Chernobyl, in Pripyat (He sensed the reactor going critical 8000 kms away). He flies into reactor 4 and splashes into the pool to sap the power from the nuclear fuel rods, as technicians stand agape. Their readings going below supercritical as we see superman holding onto the rods as he absorbs all of their power, the look on his face is of greater strain than when he stopped the tornado (as these fuel rods contain the power of hundreds if not thousands of nuclear bombs, not more energy than a tornado, but more energy than the rotational energy of a tornado). He sucks it all up.
8. He flies off into space, as the technicians cheer him! 9: He's in space heading to the Sun at Warp speeds.
9. He reaches the Sun, and gears up to discharge the energy.
10. He discharges the energy in a huge blast as the scene cuts to black.

TEARS WASHED AWAY

Song:- Carol of The Bells – Trans-Siberian Orchestra

Inspired by a Norwegian short film on YouTube dealing with sexual slavery.

RADIO START

0-0:31:- A female pianist is courted by a man to be his bride. She accepts.

0:31-0:54:- He fiercely whisks her away, to sell her into sexual slavery. Church bells are shown ringing when they do in the song. It is the season of giving. Snow is everywhere.

0:55-1:15:- As men are shown to where she is in a strange house (avoid graphic depictions of rape), as the music builds to a crescendo, a lit yellow star on a Christmas tree is shown with a panned shot.

1:16-1:29:- After her ordeal, she is shown to destress through drawing.

1:30-1:56:- As she is drawing, she sees some people walk down below her window. She furiously tries to attract their attention. As she does so, the sound attracts the man who is controlling her, he and a buddy of his grapple her and subdue her by tying her to a chair.

1:57-2:10:- They take her work and throw it out of the window as she cries broken.

2:10-2:36:- The book falls into a garbage heap, as a bunch of homeless people look for valuable items. One of them finds the book, and ruffling through the pages, he finds the drawing of "HELP!" The call and response sequence around the 2:28 mark, shows the intense focus and realization by 2 zooms filmed as such to give life to that intensity.

2:36-2:46:- The police are informed of this and they leave to free her.

2:47-3:11:- The police reach the house and they free the girl and capture the miscreants as they try to escape. She is now free (at the song's climatic juncture). Which does sound like a police siren indeed.

3:12-3:20:- As the music softens, she is shown recovering with a warm cup of cocoa near a Christmas Tree with presents. A man gently kisses her forehead as she smiles.

THE DAZZLING ONE

The scene will open in the yurt of the early years of the emperorship of the Great Kublai Khan.

Kublai Khan is in his bed quarters in his Yurt.

A Rus woman of the principality of Muscovy is sent into the bed chamber of Kublai Khan.

Instead of looking demure and deferential as most non-Mongolian of the time were, this lady, while not outwardly disrespectful of the Khan, had a certain stiffness in her body.

"Do not be worried my dear, there is nothing to be afraid of here, I'm not going to harm you. You have the word of a great Khan". Says Kublai Khan as he gently stands up and sits next to her to comfort her.

"What would you like me to do for you?"

The woman looks up, into his eyes and says,

"I would like you to ravish me."

The Khan is a bit taken aback by such a bold and forthright exclamation by the maiden, but he is not alien to it. He looks at her and smiles.

"How bold" and brushes aside her hair. The woman moves back a little.

"Why do recoil from my touch, as you would a snake?"

The woman takes off her clothes.

"I have needs, as any woman, Great Khan, as in, my husband was killed during the battle".

"Is that why my hand is as if that of a snake? Or is it because I am the dazzling one?" he says as he unfurls his hair.

The woman nods her head, as tears come from her eyes.

"Both".

He gently wipes them away.

She lunges at the Khan.

"I can show you many things".

The Khan recoils a bit, as he is thrown to his bed.

They have sex.

The guards are stoic inspite of the odd sounds that make it through, finding their way through the pockets of air in the woolen walls, escaping to their ears.

The Khan is quite satisfied as the woman leaves. He gets up and personally writes a note to send a stipend to the woman and her family.

If she is as bold and industrious in her spending as she is in bed, he will make her a Prime Minister of one his realms.

THE HELL PATROL!

Song: The Hell Patrol*Judas Priest

0-50: As the song starts with "Like wildfire, Comes roaring, Mad whirlwind, Burning the road! Black Thunder! White Lightening! Speed Demons Cry! The Hell Patrol! The Hell Patrol!"

A giant fire tornado appears in a forest, a mad whirlwind! Melting the asphalt of the road!

"Black Thunder!" "White Lightening!" A massive volcanic ash cloud from which lightening strikes!

"Speed Demons Cry!" The firefighters let out their cry!

Massive fire engines come into view rushing towards the inferno on a blackened night! As "The Hell Patrol!" is shouted!

0:50-1:29: "Night riders! Death Dealers! Storm-Bringers! Tear Up The Ground! Fists Flying! Eyes Blazing! They're Glory Bound! The Hell Patrol! The Hell Patrol!"

At "Night Riders!" the massive firefighters themselves come into view, with their monstrous bodies and massive cannons!

"Death Dealers!" One of their own dies from fire, despite their invulnerability, this angers the rest and the fight harder to douse the fire!

"Storm-Bringers!" One of them raises their hands and looks to the sky and brings down a massive thunderstorm on the equally massive forest fire!

"Tear Up The Ground!" At which they, with their bare hands rip up the Earth in front of the fire, to stop the flame!

"Fists Flying!" They punch and kick the trees to the ground, to starve the flames of their sustenance!

"Eyes Blazing!" Their eyes have burning flames exuding from their sockets. The fury of determination!

"They're Glory Bound!" They will stop at nothing, to stop the flames!

"The Hell Patrol! The Hell Patrol!" In their yellow protective gear it is revealed that they are of fire themselves! Send a fire to catch a fire! Face their Ire! Sire!

1:30-1:43: "Brutalize You! Neutralize You! Gonna Go For The Throat As You Choke! Then They'll Vaporapeize You! Terrorize You! Pulverize You! Gonna Cut To The Bone As They Paratamize You!"

"Brutalize You! Neutralize You!" That's what they do to you, you fucking fire!

They pull a person out from the hungry licking wall of flames!

"Gonna Go For The Throat As You Choke! Then They'll Vaporapeize You!"

They stab the throat of the person they pulled as they're on the ground to carry out a field tracheotomy! Then they oxygenate!

"Terrorize You! Pulverize You! Gonna Cut To The Bone As They Paratamize You!"

They blow out the flames near another person, who has gangrene! And they cut the bone to amputate as they paramedicalize you!

1:44-2:46: So Much Saving!

2:47-3:36: "Chrome Monsters! Steel Warriors! Soul Stealers! Ripping Out Hearts! They're Devil Dogs! The Hell patrol! The Hell Patrol!"

"Chrome Monsters! Steel Warriors!" Titan Guardians! They become of steel! Shining steel! Much more monstrous!

"Soul Stealers!" They preserve the souls of the fallen in glass jars! "Ripping Out Hearts!" Cardiac Surgery! Replacing them with better hearts! "They're Devil Dogs!" They're hellhounds powering through the crowd!

"The Hell Patrol! The Hell Patrol!" Gonna Cut To The Bone And Cauterize You!

THE N WORD

Inspired by a NUA (Norwich University of Arts) film of a story of a person of a mixed heritage.

A black & white montage of scenes take place. Authoritarian leaders are shown doing authoritarian things. Juxtaposed with supremacists carrying out acts of racially motivated violence. The focus shifts to a “white” supremacist carrying out an act of racial incitement. The black and white montage ends with a similar but older looking man sitting by what seems to be by himself on a sofa staring off into the distance.

His face turns to the right, lights up and then looks concerned. As his young daughter runs up and hurls herself at him. He takes her into his arms and cradles her. She is revealed to be mixed (I know that I like subtlety and it is important, but I just needed to emphasize some important things like in my script about climate change).

“Daddy they keep calling me names in school. Yesterday they called me the N word”.

Her mother comes in and sits down next to them, the father and the mother share a quick glance of concern.

“Who are they” the mom asks.

Not looking away from her torso, the girl replies,

“Three guys and one girl”.

Still cradling his daughter he says,

“Don’t worry about it dear, tomorrow I will talk to them”.

“Don’t worry about it?! What the fuck, dad?”

The parents are seemingly more taken aback by their daughter using a swear word, than the previous incident.

“Every day they mock me and make fun of me and I just want to hurt them and kill them!”

She hits her dad and struggles.

“You don’t care! None of you care! You keep saying things, but you don’t do them, you are liers! Liers! (she pronounces it this way) Let go off (not a spelling error, people sound weird when they are angry) me!”

She struggles but her dad holds her tighter and her mother comes and holds them both.

Their daughter starts crying and hot tears fall down her face, as her mouth is shut tight. And so are her eyes, as she nuzzles into her father's chest and takes deep breaths.

"I am sorry dad and mom". She whispers.

"Nothing to be sorry about". They say almost in unison, quietly.

The next day, the father goes to the school and though intuition, finds the children who were bullying his daughter.

He goes up to them and finds them studying together.

"Are you the ones hurting my daughter?"

He says curtly.

They all jump at the sound of his voice and they look up nervously at him, waiting with baited breath to see what he will do next.

He sits down next to them and asks them about why they were picking on his daughter.

"We weren't picking on you daughter, Mr."

"Don't lie to me, my daughter took a picture of you and showed it to me."

The uncomfortable and strained expression on their faces, couple with their uneasy glances at each other, gives them away.

"Why were you bullying my daughter and calling her by horribly racist terms?"

"We promise we won't do it again!" One of them says.

"Now whether you are taking out your troubles on her, or whether you're doing it for shits and giggles, I would like you to stop harassing my daughter, please.

Otherwise, I will be forced to go to the principal with your picture."

They nod in understanding.

"Good, I'm glad you understand. Stay like you are, children, study hard, work hard, become something good. Don't become assholes, it's not good. It'll be the worst for you."

He gets up without saying another word, leaving them to ruminate in their thoughts.

He goes home and finds his wife teaching their daughter. He embraces them and informs them that her bullying is over.

THIS MOMENT

Song: This Moment-Disturbed

Inspired by and derived from the story "Birthday Reflections" by BlueTitan, . Chapter 10: Love Hate Relationship

As beastboy and the emotion creeped up behind the jagged wall, they caught a glimpse of Rage. She expressed relief that Rage was distracted and so they could stay out of sight till they reached the other side. Beastboy had disappeared. He'd creeped up to go towards

Rage. He approached her altar where she was chained, from the left. Seeing this her heart caught in her throat. But she was too paralyzed by fear to do anything, but she wanted to also see what he was doing. She called out to him softly. He heard, but he went further still.

As he was climbing upto where she was chained. He looked up to catch a glimpse of the giant and menacing statue of Trigon looming far above him. For a moment he could've sworn that one of the eyes of the statue glinted, almost as if it was trying to look at him without moving (similar to how GORT's eyes move to scan his surroundings and track objects in the 2008 remake of the 'The Day The Earth Stood Still'). This caused him to miss his footing and in doing so, he kicked a stone. As it rattled across the floor, he hoped that Rage wouldn't hear him.

No such luck.

Seeing this the emotion's heart stopped. Having an entity made of pure negative emotion is no laughing matter (although it would be for Happy).

Beastboy stops trying to hide himself, and he approaches Rage. "Uh, Hi"

Rage looked fierce with her four red eyes literally on fire. Her teeth gritted with such force that you would think that she could break her own jaws just by snapping.

Rage just looks at him, but doesn't say anything. She's stopped growling and screaming and hurting herself.

And her fire has reduced in intensity a bit. It's no longer a flamethrower but a crackling fire.

"I know what it's like to be chained like an animal. But maybe if you behaved more, Raven wouldn't have to treat you like this" he says, as he approaches her more gingerly.

Rage just slowly tracks him, and loosens her arms to her sides, as he gently moves his hand to touch her face.

Rage's head swiftly moves and bites hard down on Beastboy's hand. His bones don't crack, but her sharp teeth easily reach the bone, that's far stronger than any human bite.

Inspite of the excruciating pain, beastboy manages to smile at her. And she freezes into place as his other hand softly caresses her cheek. Having never felt softness like this, the gesture makes her stop biting and instead she proceeds to gently lick his hand, like a puppy who's just realized that it did something wrong.

"DON'T THINK MUCH OF THIS. I LOATHE ALL, I DESPISE ALL" Rage says curtly.

(Rage's voice sounds like a menacing version of 'Death' from 'Terry Pratchett's The Hogfather'.)

Beast boy is taken aback by her voice.

"BUT MOST OF ALL WHAT I HATE IS, IS THAT I CAN'T HATE YOU" She continues.

"I-" But before beastboy can reply, the giant statue of Trigon springs to life. As it moves, the very ground beneath them shakes. The emotion behind the wall jumps out and runs towards Beastboy and Rage. The statue is heading for Beastboy. "It's now or never to destroy Raven completely, and now she's brought her loverboy straight to me. Ha ha ha ha!"

He reaches down to grab beastboy, as Rage shouts, "UNBIND ME!"

Beastboy transforms into Tyrannosaur and breaks the chains holding Rage to her post. Rage looks towards the other emotion and says, "LOVE, I NEED YOU TO JOIN WITH ME!"

Beastboy just looks at love and mouths "love?" Love just shrugs as she runs towards Rage. And they fuse. In the meantime, all the other emotions, knowledge, happy, brave, timid, lust and fear run towards portals to Rage's realm. It's now or never if they wish to destroy Trigon's influence in Raven's mind.

Trigon reaches to grab Tyranno-Beastboy. But then Beastboy morphs into a Spinosaur and towers over Trigon. For the first time in his life, Trigon has to look up to someone.

Beastboy snaps at Trigon's head and has his head within his jaws, beastboy realizes his mistake just in time and pushes trigon away, as he dodges Trigon's death beam by morphing into a fly. All the other Raven's run towards the LOVE-RAGE hybrid and fuse with her to form white Raven.

Meanwhile in the real world, Raven freezes while trying to capture the robbers in the bank. As she falls unconscious and turns white for some reason, to everyone's astonishment. The robbers take this opportunity to shoot Raven in the leg, but Cyborg jumps to her rescue and the bullet bounces off of his armour.

White Raven starts to fight Trigon as 'This Moment' starts to play.

It's quite the titanic fight. Death beams and Raven's white power beams flashing across and hitting each other.

One of Raven's powerful strikes almost hits Trigon, but when he blocks it, it's too late to fully stop it, and his elbow hits himself and creates a small break in himself. He grabs Raven by the throat and starts absorbing her power, as she tries to break away, Beastboy flies into the gap and reaches Trigon's centre and transforms into a Spinosaur and destroys Trigon, as Raven throws off Trigon's now severed arms, which were on her neck. She defuses and all the other emotions come apart.

(The song ends)

Rage collapses from fatigue and falls down to the ground crying from relief as Trigon's malicious influence leaves her. Happy, love and all the other emotions go to hug her tightly. There don't seem to be any difference between any of the emotions. It's just a bunch of old friends together again, 'cept they all look like Raven.

Beastboy runs in and joins the big hug.

In the real world, Raven wakes up in the Titan tower. "Raven, are you okay, friend?" says Starfire.

"You gave us quite a scare today, Raven", Robin adds.

"Now that you're awake, help us find beastboy so that I can pummel some sense in him" Cyborg says smacking his fist into his hand.

"I'll get up, I'll get him" Raven says.

Then she starts to have tears in her eyes and feels a tightness in her chest. But she starts to smile and laugh so hard, it's almost like she's Beastboy. And then she starts to cry as she laughs. As they all come in to hug her.

"Friend, what makes you laugh and cry at the same time?" Starfire whispers in her ear. "Oh Starfire" Raven gives her a kiss on the lips.

"Isn't this a sign of affection on your planet as well?" "Yes, it's very common between people"

"Everyone, I'm free of Trigon's influence" "What?!" Everyone says.

Cyborg's jaw falls to the floor, as he reaches up to grab it and reattach it. "How?"

"Beastboy"

"I'll go get him"

Raven prances off into the distance, leaving all of them gawking at her with their mouths open, with Cyborg reaching down to pick up his jaw again.

Raven enters her room, and is not cognizant of its grimness. And picks up her 'nevermore' mirror.

In her mind, the emotions together bring beastboy to the exit of Raven's mind. The forbidden door.

"This is it Beastboy" they say in unison.

It's a little creepy. All the Ravens give beastboy a kiss and hug at the sametime.

The door opens and beastboy is pulled out by the vortex and materializes infront of everybody.

"Uh.. hey guys!" Beastboy waves at them.

They wave back with their mouths open, as they reach down to pick up their jaws. 'Cept Cyborg's because he's already experienced this.

"So, beastboy went into my mind, and with the other mes' he destroyed Trigon for good. I had sent him in as my gift for his birthday to really tell him how I feel, I had no idea that he had a return gift". She says as she leans in to hug him.

Everyone's still staring.

"Raven's happy?!"' "Raven's telling jokes?!"

"Raven's hugging beastboy?!"

"I'm going to do a scan on this imposter!" Raven laughs and says, "Cyborg! It's me!" "Prove it"

In Cyborg's mind, a voice says, "I sent Robin's picture to all the places you wanted it too"

Immediately Cyborg's face lights up and he hugs Raven real hard, "That's our Raven"

After Robin's humiliation at the hands of the Titans East, all the male villains and the female villains who he locked up and Cyborg. Beastboy and Raven walk out of the conference room together while holding hands.

TURBO DRIVER

Song: Turbo Lover (Remastered-Live)-Judas Priest

A movie on the game, Driver: San Francisco.

For this movie, check out the YouTube video "This is what a 'Second-Person Game' Video Game Would Look Like".

This sequence is inspired from Driver: San Francisco Chapter 6 #6 story-The Target.

"Ordell", says Leila looking at him.

"It's time to kill yourself, not many people get the privilege".

The race begins, as Ordell rushes to catch himself.

Music begins.

0-13: Tires burn. (Close up on the tires).

0:14-1:23:- The Race Begins (Night-Atmospheric palette)

POV is from Ordell's view in the SUV.

1:24-2:03:- They head into oncoming traffic, bobbing and weaving, pedestrians on the sidewalk leap out of the way, as they climb the curb.

2:04-2:06:- In really cool, "Need For Speed" style, the camera tracks the wheels of the pursuing SUV.

Of course, throughout the course of this chase scene, Tanner's Dodge Challenger stays obstinately infront of and away from the pursuant vehicle.

2:07-2:56:- It seems as though "Ordell" is getting closer to 'Tanner's" car. And in fact at the 2:41 mark of the song, Tanner's car scrapes against a concrete block, in a daring maneuver that almost brings him under "Ordell's" grasp.

Of this rendition of the song, at the 2:41 mark, play the "closer" lyric from Turbo Driver (Remastered) (The Remastered-live performance has it at the 2:31 mark).

2:56-2:58:- At this point, they both hit their Nitrous boost, as they shift to overdrive!

2:59-3:23:- Their speed is so intense, it blurs the sky, the cars they all seem to pass them by, as if they have some magical physics. Even thought they're in oncoming traffic, everything moves out of their way, even the dustbins fly out of their way.

3:25-3:48:- They reach a long bridge over water, on the right side of the road, they come face to face with one another. Tanner looking at himself (and Jones), through "Ordell's" eyes.

3:49-4:38:- "Ordell" now side-swipes Tanner's car and his car goes into a tail spin. He controls the spin, with a drift down the turn of a flyover and steadies the car.

At the guitar rift, the race continues straight, with the SUV trailing close behind. Leila is seen threatening "Ordell" to do better.

4:38-4:41:- At the guitar riff, the police blockade now comes into view.

4:42-5:05:- Tanner does a dangerous move, he drifts his rear into the SUV's front and "Ordell" is unable to counter, and his car spins out of control. The compensating measure by "Ordell" of ramming his front into the SUV spins both cars out chaotically.

5:05-5:34:- The cars spin out just at the start of the police barricades, as the edges of both the cars touch the police vehicles. The camera pans away, as cops surround the Black SUV.

ULTIMATE

(Song: Ultimate-Denzel Curry, bitch I'm beast, nigga', you fucking with me?)

Apologiez if this is to absurdist, and you don't get it (I care. A less than a lot, but more than a little drizzle, 'tis butt a spittle from the sky).

Timestamps:

0-0:12 (intro), 2. 12-31 (intro), 3. 32-1:30 (Verse 1), 4. 1:31-1:47(Chorus), 5. 1:48-2:38

(Worse 2), 6. 2:38-2:54 (Chorus), 7. 2:54-3:08 (outro).

Follow the lyrics, but this will follow as it sounds.

Basically, the rapper will follow the lyrics, but the music video will look like how it sounds to someone who doesn't know the lyrics. This is gonna be hard. Now I know it! Now I don't!

Aiieeee! Now you know why artists have to be mentally ill?! It's because of this, mon ami. Lyrics: /Denzel-curry-ultimate-lyrics

1. (Get Freddie Wong? For reference see the video, 'Mexican Standoff, ft. Freddie Wong', RocketJump). The vocalization which sounds like "Freddy J, Listen up". The camera pans into his face as he looks up. At the "Cha-Ching" sound, a typewriter slides back to the start of a new line.
2. Man starts rapping with his posse. "I am the one, don't weigh a ton, don't need a gun to get respect up on the street". He's a fat guy now, he doesn't need a gun to get respect on the street. The camera shifts at "Under The Sun", the Sun is shown, as a Bastard Son pops a Glock to feed himself and family, which he points at a car window (as he walks up to it). At the line which sounds like, "By any means, your enemies, my enemies, we work them up like a

canteen", our rapper (he's slim now, like fatboy slim) shakes an empty and open canteen. "Faith". Hmmm? "Don't have a face, so now you like open the gates". Nobody has a face, and now, you like, open the gates.

3. The line which sounds like, "Great, levitate like I levitate". As he says this a guy next to him levitates. "Hey, young boy had to penetrate". As a boy punches his pencil through a piece of blank paper effortlessly. "Hey, young boy, done got a case". As a court file hits a boy in the face. "Doctor says he's a gonna stay (huh?)". A man is shown strapped to an electric chair, with a doctor standing next to him (I know you got a job miss Cheney, but your husband's heart problems complicatin'. Different video, Eminem video, but it fits right? Just a reference, no need to include it). "Through a nigga' harder than the head of a state (huh?)". What it says. You over there! Throw a nigga' harder than the head of a state. "Ultimate, Ultimate, you are the opposite". Rapper holds up a negative sign and points to it. "Chop your shit; chop your esophagus (esophagus)". Chop your shit. Chop the esophagus of a human mock up made of ballistic gel (with a kitana/samurai sword). "Bitches Be Boppin' it, drop it in her esophagus". Camera points to a bitch (female dog) as she drops to the ground. Drop a sausage in her esophagus (absurdist humour and suggestive humour, yay!). "She is so nasty, in public she classy, perhaps she's able to swallow it; Girl, I could make you a star, then I put her ass on Apollo, bitch". Ah, here, we show a pig in mud (female?), she shows her class in public (upper, middle, lower, destitute, Class/Section/Room/Grade 8E?), perhaps the dog is able to swallow the sausage. A little girl stands next to him, looking at him, as he makes her a star (wire-frame, crayon or fusion?), then he puts her ass (donkey, you dummy) on the Saturn V rocket. "Narcissist, part time an arsonist (flame)".

   Walks down a street with homes, rapping, looks into a mirror, fires a flamethrower, fills the screen (flame!). "Rippin' through cartilage, I'm the hardest, bitch". Slaps a person in the neck (the right-handside), holds up and looks at a bucky-ball (Carbon C-60, the mockup of a molecule of carbon nanotubes, named after Buckminsterfullerene, the guy who discovered it), and then he looks at the dog (the female dog). "Sarcophagus". Raps from inside a sarcophagus as a mummy (whoever's mummy) (damn!). "Dearly, Departed". Rapping in a church, during a funeral, on a podium, as the reverend. What's he saying? Jeez. "So that I'm living so harmonious (eh), feeling like Spartacus, the ultimate". I got nothing, you? "I'm the best, it's no politics, bitch I'm ultimate". What can I say? He's says all this to the dog, as he's looking straight into the camera (close up/not a sponsorship, bitch). There's no politics (blows up/bans politics). Bitch, I'm ultimate.

4. Repeat 2 (Chorus).

   "Ultimate, Infinite". Buzz Lightyear (of star command) anyone? "Photosynthesis". Plant that motherfucker. "Parenthesis". Holds up parentheses.

   "Temporary, very scary, if I feel like Dirty Harry, just might bust a bitch, hissy fit". Points a

5. 357 towards the ground at the camera. Makes a bust of the dog. Hissy fit, puts his hand up in a questioning gesture. "Chop a bitch nigga' up, when I sever shit". Chops a bitch nigga' up again. "Enter the cosmic, flow like a prophet, lyrical toxic". Enters the cosmic. Flows like a prophet from a cave, vomits out toxic garbage, which makes everyone epic (ultimate?). "Flow like a foreigner, Imma torture her". Flows like a waterer, tries to torture her, by not

responding to her (a dog in heat). "Corridor, Overlord, I'm an animorph, sorcerer". Hallway becomes him, him becomes a God who snaps the Universe into existence (which is the corridor, :-D) and then transforms into a half-fish, half-man on land. "Bitch I'm a beast, nigga' you tell me you fucking with me". Transforms into the abomination from 'Darkest Dungeon' as he thumps his muscular and most lupine chest. Pushes NigaHiga back. "K-I-N- G, claim you're the hardest, but I disagree". Becomes a king, smashes a diamond with a hammer (you'll never be as hard as me). "Bladder loves something, and get a degree, this were infamous, so RIP". Holds up a pitcher of water, gets frozen, goes to bathroom, gets shot in the face and goes on a fucking gravediggin' spree. "Are you vederci? Bitches looking thirsty, like they're dirty, mandatory". Are you vederci? The bust of the dog comes after him being thirsty (weeping angels anyone?). Pigs are dirty mandatory, show a whole sty of them being dirty.

6. Repeat 2 (Chorus).
7. Outro. Do a random hip-hop jive for fun (for reference look at the ending of the video: 'Black violin – A-flat').

VAN OPENER

One woman says coyly to another woman, "What are you going to do to me?" The other woman spreads her labia open with her tongue, and humms.

The other woman moans in pleasure.

The woman talks into her vagina and says, "I'm going to spreadeagle you, you minx".

The other woman says, "Whatever you're saying, say it louder, you know that I can't hear you, when you eat with your mouth open".

WHO DO YOU VODOO BITCH?

Song: Who Do You Voodoo, Bitch?! Sam B (ft. Papa Shongo and Baron Samedi), Dead Island OST.

Note, Before The Script: At every point where he says, 'Who Do You Voodoo Bitch?" He waves a finger (sort of like the girl in 'Skrillex-First Of The Year') and he breaks the limbs of a woman. With each limb broken, move to the bones, with the pain evident in her face and eyes in every relevant shot. With each bone broken, the zombies get closer, and as they reach her, before the song ends, you can see her terrified and bloodied face, as many zombie hands cover her face, as she's dragged down. Sam B looks like a zombie, whenever he says, 'Sam B'.

0:02-0:11: He's speaking to the camera. Sam B looks like Mr. T.

0:12-0:42: Graphically depict everything that he's saying. 0:44-1:03: Who Do You Voodoo, Bitch?

1:04: Ha ha ha ha ha!

1:25-1:43: Graphically depict whatever he's saying.

1:44-1:52: 1:45, 1:46 Laughter, Fill In the blanks for yourself. 1:53-2:15: Who Do You Voodoo, Bitch?

2:16-2:22: Guess who the zombies feast on?

This is basically what I told my therapist. That writing a story about hateful violence, as opposed to other forms of violence (triumphant, for example), doesn't get very far, with me, atleast, as there's not very far to go with it. It doesn't leave me feeling very well. But, I gave it a try, and I did feel better, but this is probably not a very healthy outlet for that hatred. But, it's definitely better than somebody's skull. Or your skull, for that matter. You knew that I'm a psycho, told you I'm a psycho, 'cause really I'm a psycho, Violent

Schizophrenia, you know that I'm gonna get ya, why, why, why, why, why, why, why? I told ya, I told ya, didn' I tell ya? Why-ha ha ha ha!

And guess what? That lovely peace of art right there? That's from a song, the Happy Song. Poets of the Fall. Lovely.

Note: Changed 'Bitch' for woman. I have female friends, and even though I'm trying to get all my hatred out in one story (impossible, I know), I thought I'll just let the subtlety of the song do the talking. Anyways, the postscript of 'Star Crystals' is more irreverent and vicious, as I do not have many theist friends, but nevertheless, I extend my apology to them. If you're Christian, perhaps, don't read the postscript of 'Star Crystals'. If you're Muslim, don't read the postscript of that, same for the Jews. Or do read it, if you want.

I don't know.

WHY DO YOU THINK I WEAR RED, COMRADE?

FADE IN:

In Front Of A Screen-Day 1

Music Plays From Kalinka (Red Army Choir) 2:03-2:10

WE OPEN as Red Santa opens his arms in tune with the music and sits down in front of a screen to speak to the other red Santa. The music stops.

Remain:

Still In Front Of The Screen-Day 2

The Two Santas (Played By The Same Person/Or Different People) Are Sitting Facing Each Other.

RED SANTA 1(COM)

Hello Santa, here to proselytize me into the cause of the capitalists? Red Santa 2 looks incredulous.

RED SANTA 2(CAP)

Looks to Santa 1, phuh, we both want the same thing workplace democracy.

RED SANTA 1(COM)

Yes, but the way that we both want it is different. I want no money to be present in this benefit system of mine and the elves should have control over everything.

RED SANTA 2(CAP)

Yes, well your system requires constant coal usage and that is causing climate change!

RED SANTA 1(COM)

Well your solar panels and "environmental ethics" (in quotations) require my coal to be traded with you!

RED SANTA 2(CAP)

Yes! And you make this job more difficult by not having any money!

RED SANTA 1(COM)

Yes! But, my rotund friend, that's communism!

No it's not!

RED SANTA 2(CAP)

RED SANTA 1(COM)

Yes it is!

RED SANTA 2(CAP)

You can always do what the collectivist anarchists do and have money, it would make all our jobs easier, mate (does a collective gesture, signifying **us**). How am I supposed to pay all those elf benefits without money?

ELF 1(CAP)

Sweet, squeaky elven voice

Santa! Santa! We need those food stamps!

RED SANTA 2(CAP)

Points to the little cutie-patootie elf

See what I mean? My whole economic system is based on money! I have to feed all my little cute muchkins! Don't I? ***Affectionately pulls the cheek of Elf 1 (CAP) (off screen to the right-handside) ***

ELF 1(CAP)

Makes cute, loving expression

RED SANTA 1(COM)

Heart melts Awww! Wait! I know what you're doing! You cappy! You're pandering to my emotions, well it's not going to work! And don't speak to me of anarchists! Pah! Socialist traitors! Foolish idealists!

RED SANTA 2(CAP)

Well, okay how about this (conciliatory)? You use money just for trading with me, I give you the solar panels, the environmental ethics, you clean up your coal act, I pay benefits to my elves, and we all win once coal finishes since we all will have renewable energy in the end and clean up our act, how's that for a negotiation?

RED SANTA 1(COM)

And what about the naughties? How do I punish those little gremlins (just his head forward and sideways in a comically aggressive manner)?

RED SANTA 2(CAP)

(Leans forward) Comrade, two words, (puts up two fingers), coconut chocolates.

RED SANTA 1(COM)

(Laughs boisterously and then clasps hands with RED SANTA 2)

RED SANTA 2(CAP)

I think that our word is good enough.

RED SANTA 1(COM)

I guess that that makes me a collectivist anarchist now.

RED SANTA 2(CAP)

And I guess that that keeps me popular! There aren't any elections, but I don't want all my elves to go you!

RED SANTA 1(COLL ANC)

Indeed, and not mine to you! (Laughs boisterously again)

RED SANTA 2(CAP)

(Sighs) So what now?

RED SANTA (COLL ANC)

Now This! (Presses a play button) (off screen to the bottom)

FADE OUT:

END SCREEN-DAY-MUSIC-ROTEM HECHT-WORKERS AND RESOURCES SOVIET REPUBLIC OST-WORKER'S

MARCH-1:13-1:23 3

End title card with the following words: "Sorry, I know that it's all communist music, but don't worry, you can take solace in the fact that it was all made in a capitalist world with market forces, comrades".

RED SANTA 2(CAP) (V.O.)

Why does the commy have to be the first to go?

RED SANTA 1(COLL ANC) (V.O.)

Because this was written by a socialist.

RED SANTA 2(CAP) (V.O.)

Where are all the Caps?

RED SANTA 1(COLL ANC) (V.O.)

They're too busy making explosions for money! (Laughs explosively and points fingers!)

RED SANTA 2 (CAP) (V.O)

Hey! Don't be mean!

RED SANTA 1(COLL ANC) (V.O.)

C'mon, let's go, this sketch is over.

BOTH SANTAS SPEAK 4

FADE IN:

RED SANTA 1 AND 2 (MIXED ECON AND CIVICS)

Merry Christmas to All! And to all a Good Night! (Clasping of hands)

WUB WUB

Saints Row IV: Datsik an Excision-Vindicate

0-0:35:- The music starts, as a young man is attracted towards a dubstep gun in a shop and picks it up. He then walks with it out to a lovely sunny day.

0:35-1:09:- He charges up his cannon, as everyone looks at him strangely, prepare for the bass drop.

1:10-1:34:- Everybody and everything starts to dance, as the very fabric of reality warps! The Dubstep Gun does its wub-wubs through a mouth instead of a speaker! Beat-Boxing!

1:35-1:36:- An an iron girder falls to the ground!

1:37-2:02:- More dubstep, more dancin'! Dancing! As the music builds up and reaches a crescendo.

2:03-2:09:- The whole world starts dancing! (We can even show various people dancing, even serious ones like Khomeini, although the part below might make us think twice due to a Fatwa!)

2:10:- A dog barks!

2:11-2:19:- More dancing! With slow motion. 2:20:- Someones head asplodes into pink confetti!!

2:20-2:26:- More dancing, more dog barks, more slow motion!! 2:28-2:39:- More intense Dubstep dancing!

2:40-2:55:- A shadow looms over everyone and the Earth. As the music builds. An asteroid is heading for Earth! Everyone connects their speakers to the Dubstep!

2:56-3:29:- The music builds, as everyone waits with baited breath! As the Asteroid gets closer!

3:30-3:54:- The Earth has a mouth, the Earth is Dubstep!

The Asteroid Dances and breaks up! Reality warps! Drop The Bass!! Dubstep!! 3:55:- All the iron girders drop!!

3:56-4:04:- Wub Wub!!

4:05-4:25:- The Dubstep winds down, as the Dubstep cannon winds down and is left alone in the shop, its mission complete!! Wub! Wub!

9 789356 211872

Printed at Repro India Ltd.